The Zimmer doctrine
F Coo Corps #11   TE0021

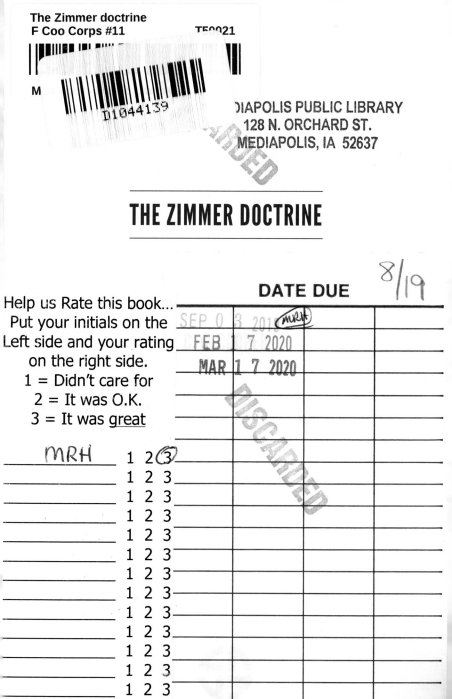

D1044139

M

DIAPOLIS PUBLIC LIBRARY
128 N. ORCHARD ST.
MEDIAPOLIS, IA 52637

THE ZIMMER DOCTRINE

DATE DUE   8/19

Help us Rate this book...
Put your initials on the
Left side and your rating
on the right side.
1 = Didn't care for
2 = It was O.K.
3 = It was <u>great</u>

		SEP 0 8 2019 (MRH)	
		FEB 1 7 2020	
		MAR 1 7 2020	

MRH   1 2 ③
_____   1 2 3
_____   1 2 3
_____   1 2 3
_____   1 2 3
_____   1 2 3
_____   1 2 3
_____   1 2 3
_____   1 2 3
_____   1 2 3
_____   1 2 3
_____   1 2 3
_____   1 2 3
_____   1 2 3
_____   1 2 3

PRINTED IN U.S.A.

"THE ZIMMER DOCTRINE"

Book 11 of the Corps Justice Series
Copyright © 2015, 2018 C. G. Cooper Entertainment. All Rights Reserved
Author: C. G. Cooper

**GET A FREE COPY OF THE CORPS JUSTICE PREQUEL
SHORT STORY, *GOD-SPEED*, JUST FOR SUBSCRIBING AT
CG-COOPER.COM**

This is a work of fiction. Characters, names, locations and events are all
products of the author's imagination. Any similarities to actual events or real
persons are completely coincidental.
Any unauthorized reproduction of this work is strictly prohibited.

Warning: This story is intended for mature audiences and contains
profanity and violence.

DEDICATIONS

To my loyal group of *Novels Live* warriors, thanks for your undying enthusiasm. Keep pushing me up the hill.

To our amazing troops serving all over the world, thank you for your bravery and service.

And to the United States Marine Corps: Keep taking the fight to the enemy.
Semper Fidelis

TECHNION- ISRAEL INSTITUTE OF TECHNOLOGY

Haifa, Israel

AUGUST 24TH, 10:38AM

A rare curse escaped Dr. Aviel Nahas's lips as the needle-nose pliers pinched his left index finger. The Israeli scientist-turned-inventor flung the tool across the room, barely missing a neat row of cork-topped vials. He winced at the clatter while he chided himself for being so rash. He'd never had a temper. Until recently, he'd never once yelled at another human being in his adult life.

Dr. Nahas exhaled and tried to concentrate on his work. The last two months had been the most strenuous of his fifty-two years of life. Living under this constant anxiety wouldn't help him complete his current project in the time allotted. Earlier that day, upon looking in the mirror, it appeared he'd accumulated a new crop of overzealous gray hair. And for what?

The grant provided was substantial, the largest in his career, but the toll it was taking on his health and the time it was stealing from his other projects...

He shook his head and sighed. Such was the price of

doing business with the Israeli government. His colleagues had warned him, but he had not listened. Looking back, Dr. Nahas knew that his own ego, a thing that had rarely reared itself during his distinguished career, was now threatening to induce a nervous breakdown.

His once dead-steady hands felt clumsy and alien to him. His world-renowned brain flitted from fear to fear like some buzzing insect rather than staying on task.

He owed this change in his temperament to those government slave drivers and especially that bastard Colonel Osman. The man didn't have a clue about proper protocol. He insisted on calling at odd hours, pressing him with strange questions, and treating Dr. Nahas like a lowly soldier. He was Dr. Aviel Nahas!

For the hundredth time, Dr. Nahas debated filing a grievance. Maybe someone would listen and get Osman off his back. He didn't need to be micro-managed. The stress of constant scrutiny would only serve to impede the speed with which he could complete his work.

But he was a quiet man, not one to make waves. With a heavy dose of reluctance, Dr. Nahas got up from his stool and went to fetch the discarded pliers. As he bent over to pick them up from the floor, the office door buzzed, signaling someone's entrance. His stomach turned at the thought of yet another snap inspection by Osman. However, when he arose it wasn't Col. Osman coming through the door.

Dr. Nahas stared at the three men standing in front of him. They were all dressed casually, their faces amiable yet unreadable. With their light complexions and sandy hair, Nahas presumed they were of European descent. He thought they looked like athletes who'd somehow, while en route to the gym, took a wrong turn and instead stumbled upon his work space.

"Can I help you?" he asked them.

"Doctor Nahas?"one of the men asked in English, rather than the usually-spoken Hebrew. He had handsome emerald eyes.

"Yes?"

"We've been sent to fetch you, Doctor."

He didn't have any meetings scheduled. Col. Osman had made sure that his only responsibility was the completion of his current endeavor.

"I am sorry, gentlemen, who are you with?" Dr. Nahas asked.

"Our employer would like a word with you concerning your research."

It was not an unreasonable request. He had wealthy businessmen asking him for a number of meetings. But this request could not have come at a worse time.

"If you could please tell your employer that I am extremely busy at the moment. I have a deadline, you see, and..."

"We know about tomorrow's deadline, Doctor."

Dr. Nahas froze. There was something in the man's eyes now, a goading, like he was toying with him.

"That is impossible. This project is..."

"Classified," the man finished for him. "We know all about it. That is what our employer would like to discuss."

He could not discuss it with anyone except Col. Osman and his people. Dr. Nahas knew that Osman would kill him if he found out that he'd broken the terms of the grant.

"You will be compensated for your time, Doctor. Now, if you please, we have a car waiting outside."

The man was courteous and he even smiled when he motioned to the door.

Dr. Nahas shook his head.

"As I said, I am very busy. Leave me your card and I

promise to contact you as soon as my work has been concluded."

He wanted the men to leave. The adrenaline had cleared his muddled mind. How had these men found out about his work? His research and development was so highly classified that even his parents were not cleared to know what he was doing.

"I am afraid I must insist," the man said, still smiling.

Dr. Nahas summoned the courage to reach for the phone. He'd extended his hand to pick up the receiver when the man firmly insisted, "Please turn around, Dr. Nahas." Then, in an abrasive tone that left no doubt as to the men's intentions, he growled, "With your hands up please, Doctor."

For the first time ever, Dr. Nahas wished that Col. Osman would show up for one of his impromptu inspections. He didn't like the man but he knew the grizzled veteran could single-handedly take care of the strangers.

When he turned to face the three men, they held pistols in their hands. Any forthcoming retort stuck in his throat as one of the men grabbed his laptop off the table.

"Now you may lower your hands, Doctor," the green-eyed man said. "Come quietly and I can promise you will not be harmed."

Dr. Nahas almost laughed despite the fear threatening to choke his air supply. All he could do was nod and gulp.

Pistols were holstered and hidden from view. The man carrying his laptop opened the door, looking first left and then right down the hallway. He gave the all-clear sign to his companions and the green-eyed man gruffly nudged Dr. Nahas to the door.

With every step, his feet felt like dead weights. Dr. Nahas wondered again if Col. Osman would make a sudden appearance, saving him from whatever fate these men and their employer had in mind.

They passed unobservant university students as they marched down the hall. No one knew him. He was a stranger, just a temporary tenant in their midst.

The four men walked out into the late summer heat. There was a dark SUV idling beside the curb. Dr. Nahas shivered. He took another look around, praying to see Col. Osman's scowling face, which never came. Dr. Aviel Nahas slid into the back of the waiting SUV, and he disappeared without receiving a second look from students or faculty rushing to escape the scorching sunlight.

DUNECREST LANE

Wild Dunes Resort

ISLE OF PALMS, SOUTH CAROLINA - AUGUST 26TH, 9:00AM

It was the same routine every Wednesday. She let herself in with the combination provided by the property management company.

She'd taken care of the current tenant for five months. It was beyond her comprehension how one person could afford the luxury of staying in a five-bedroom beachfront rental for that duration.

Only twice had she seen him. The first time he was on the rooftop porch, staring out to sea. The second time he'd been at the bedroom door. He nodded quietly and then closed the door. He was a handsome man but his eyes were hollow, bordering on haunted. His eyes reminded her of the street children she gave dollar bills to when she visited her sister in Xalapa.

Carmela's first stop was the kitchen on the third floor, adjacent to the master bedroom. As usual the place was spotless, but that didn't stop her from dusting every ledge, vacuuming every inch, and mopping the hardwoods until they shined in the sunlight.

There were no dishes to be washed, no food to be discarded. Even the refrigerator was empty. Carmela knew from months prior that someone was living in the house; however, her only clue was the neat pile of Styrofoam to-go boxes in the kitchen trashcan.

As a mother of six, she frowned with disapproval when she inspected the trash. After lifting the lids of the top two boxes, Carmela saw that the meals inside were barely touched. She made a sign of the cross and returned to her duties. Whoever this man was, he would need a mountain of prayers. Carmela decided to add him to her daily prayers.

* * *

HE'S DEAD. TRAVIS IS DEAD.

Cal Stokes lifted his head at the sound of the housekeeper's humming. It never bothered him, but then nothing bothered him anymore. It was as if the colors and tastes of the world had somehow been ripped from his being. He just didn't care. He felt completely numb.

He'd hit the road in March traveling from Charlottesville to San Diego. He then traveled to London, if for no other reason than Travis had spent time there over the years. *His cousin, Travis Haden, was dead.* The remaining branch on Cal's family tree had been forcibly removed from his life and torn from his soul by the brutality of fate.

San Diego had been a blur. He drank his way from bar to bar, often catching glimpses of times spent with Travis. Travis flirting with a girl, Travis ordering a Boilermaker, Travis laughing with his SEAL buddies. It was too much and London wasn't much better.

His bender continued across the Atlantic. He was an easy target for the London locals, drunk punks who loved to fight and draw blood. It had been too easy. They were no match. Two on one? No problem. Four on one? Fuck them. Six on one? Now, that had been the doozy. Ten stitches and a stern warning from the cops later he'd hopped on another plane, back to the States, to the only place he could think of - the beach.

Travis had loved the beach. They'd spent much of their childhood taking trips to the beach. When they were in middle and high school, they would take Cal's dad's car and hit the waves outside Camp Pendleton or they'd comb the beach for girls at Camp Lejeune. But Charleston was Travis's favorite. There he could get away and blend in with the civilian crowd.

The last vacation taken together was to the same house where Cal now resided. The management company had said it was booked for most of the summer but after Cal had offered double the going rate for the entire year the owner happily consented. The cost didn't matter; Cal could afford it.

He'd shaved his head to save time at the barber. At least that's what he'd told himself. It really was to save himself the headache of going out in public. Every time he stepped into a grocery store, he felt like everyone was looking at him. "How are you doing?" "Are you okay?" he imagined them asking.

Now he had his food delivered to the house. When he wasn't sleeping, he was sprinting barefoot over the sand until he wanted to puke, or he was swimming against the riptide until his lungs felt like they would explode.

But none of it helped. The booze had lost its taste. In fact, he hadn't touched alcohol since leaving London. Food no longer looked or tasted appealing. He ate it simply to have energy for his jogs.

Cal wondered if the day would come when he'd just lose the will to get out of bed. Sometimes he wished for that day.

It was all so empty now, like a shell of a life, a void where once there had been light.

Cal closed his eyes and tried not to think. But the thoughts came without bidding, like a neon sign blinking in a dark alley. First he had lost his parents, then Jess, and now Trav.

He's dead. Travis is dead.

* * *

"How is he, Daniel?" President Brandon Zimmer asked. He'd asked the same question twice a week for the last five months.

"He'll be okay," Daniel Briggs answered.

Daniel had been the one to follow Cal after Travis's funeral. He'd stayed in the shadows, always watching. He'd told the president that Cal knew he was near, but not once in five months had he made any attempt to contact his fellow Marine.

"How does he look?" the president asked.

"Thinner," came the sniper's honest reply.

Zimmer shook his head. He was minutes away from addressing the United Nations. It could be the pivotal speech of his career. He was supposed to be rehearsing but, just like so many times since March, the president found himself lost in thoughts of Travis Haden and Cal Stokes. Travis had been both his Chief of Staff and a good friend, and he considered Cal his best friend. They had bonded through tragedy and bloodshed, through good times and bad. Travis, Cal and Daniel had risked everything for Zimmer when everyone else had wanted to see him fail. He'd taken them for granted. Not until a terrorist's lucky shot killed Travis and the resulting grief sent Cal running did the president truly understand how integral a part they had played in his life.

He'd racked his brain trying to conceive of a way to help Cal, to pull him from his despair, but every idea seemed too contrived or not sincere enough to compensate for the loss.

"Is there anything I can do?" Zimmer asked.

"He'll come out of it," Daniel said, his even tone reminding the president that Daniel had been through the same, if not worse, and had come out okay.

"Just let me know if you need me."

"I will. Thanks for calling and good luck today."

The president chuckled, suddenly remembering that he was standing just outside the back entrance to the General Assembly.

"Thanks, I may need it."

* * *

DANIEL SMILED WHEN THE CALL ENDED. BRANDON ZIMMER was a good man. Despite his nonstop schedule, Cal was always on the president's mind. He'd offered any resources he had at his disposal including therapists, vacation homes, and anything else that might aid in returning Cal to the land of the living.

But it wasn't that easy. Daniel knew that Cal had to deal with the crippling pain in his own time and in his own way. It had only been five months. Daniel had spent years traveling from town to town before finally finding his peace.

He would not rush Cal's recovery. He would not push.

He would wait, and he would pray. The answers would come and, when they did, Daniel would be there.

THE UNITED NATIONS

New York City, New York

AUGUST 26TH, 10:58AM

"Mr. President?"

Zimmer looked up from the phone in his hand to find his press secretary, Bob Lundgren, staring at him like he'd been trying to get the president's attention.

"Sorry, Bob, what did you say?"

"I asked if you were ready to take the stage," Lundgren said, barely able to keep his annoyance out of his tone. He could really be a pain in the ass, but the former news anchor was damned good at his job. "They're ready for you."

President Zimmer nodded absently.

"Yeah, give me a..."

Lundgren waited for the president to finish.

Zimmer felt tingles running up and down his body at the revelation that had just flashed in his brain. He grunted.

"Sir, is everything...?" Lundgren started.

Zimmer waved away his concern.

"I'm good. Look, there's been a change in plans. Do you have some paper and a pen?"

Concern creased Lundgren's face but he snapped his fingers and one of his ever-roving staffers handed over a stack of note cards and a pen. Zimmer grabbed them first and hurried over to a side table to jot down his thoughts before they disappeared into thin air.

"Mr. President, could you tell me what you have in mind?"

If there was anything Bob Lundgren hated, it was a change to his carefully-orchestrated plans. This was his show. He'd personally rewritten the speech. It was Zimmer's first address in front of the United Nations. Not only would it help establish the tone for the remainder of the president's term, but also it held the promise to jump start his re-election campaign. In light of a looming re-election in little over a year, any prime time viewership they could obtain was gold.

President Zimmer didn't look up from his writing, but said, "Tell them to turn the teleprompters off. In fact, see if they'll take them offstage."

"But, sir, the speech..."

"Change of plans, Bob."

Zimmer finally looked up and almost laughed at the look of complete exasperation on Lundgren's face but that would have been cruel. Instead, he patted his press secretary on the shoulder and said, "The good news is that you'll be kept plenty busy after I've delivered my speech."

THE UNITED NATIONS STAFF WAS JUST REMOVING THE teleprompters when President Zimmer walked on stage. He held a single note card in his left hand, and he looked quite presidential in his blue suit, white dress shirt and red tie, and the American flag pinned upon his lapel. He had more gray hair than the day he'd taken office, but he wore it well, only adding to his look of stateliness.

He knew that most of the world didn't have a clue what to think about him. A Massachusetts Democrat, Zimmer had done anything but toe the party line. Some had taken to calling him "The Hawk" while others called him a traitor to the cause. It was time to dispel any doubts of how his presidency would be remembered. He would blend his two sides, and he had Travis and Cal to thank for the inspiration.

At the moment, re-election was the farthest thing from his mind. When he reached the podium, greeted by a chorus of polite clapping, Zimmer patted his right pocket. Inside was the only memento he'd taken from his former Chief of Staff's office, Travis's SEAL Trident pin. Zimmer smiled to the crowd, realizing that many in the assemblage would soon look at him quite differently.

"Be with me, Trav", Zimmer thought.

He glanced first at the note card lying on the podium and then out at the crowd gathered before him. They were expecting a speech on the global economy and America's plan to be at the forefront of tariff relaxation in addition to more open lanes of trade. *Not this time.*

"Ladies and gentlemen, delegates, world leaders, and friends, I want to sincerely thank you for allowing me the privilege of addressing this distinguished assembly. It seems like only yesterday that I stood at the top of those stairs in the far corner, as a young boy, and I watched in wonder as President Reagan addressed this very room." Zimmer shook his head at the memory. "Reagan was a master orator and a skilled politician who understood the value of a well-placed word. In addition, he personified the values of honesty and friendship. Now, I will never pretend to have his skills in front of an audience, but I think I have learned the need for honesty and valued friendships. I've been lucky enough to have friends in my life who have taught me more about morality and ethics than I ever could have learned in a class-room. That is why I am here today. Most of you were expecting to hear a speech about global trade, and my administration is working tirelessly to further invigorate the global economy. However, I believe there is a more pressing issue I feel compelled to tackle first."

He could hear the clicking of cameras, saw whispers between delegates, and sensed the mounting tension in the room. He'd never felt so sure about anything in his life. He felt like he was floating above the room, in complete command of his thoughts.

"We live in a world of a thousand colors, shapes and creeds. War mingles with impossible beauty. Lives are lost as new communities are built. As citizens of the world, we must come together to build a global community built on acceptance and openness. I stand before you today to renew my pledge to both our current and future allies. We will stand with you, protect you, and train you. However, we will not be manipulated – by anyone. Like a corporation investing in another business, we reserve the right to ensure that our money, our resources, and the precious lives of our men and women in uniform are optimally utilized. What does this mean? As soon as I leave this building, my administration will begin a top-down analysis of our continuing aid, both monetary and military, to countries around the world. I will task my leaders to provide me honest assessments of three things. First, are we getting a positive return on our investment? Is the change reaped commensurate with the aid package being provided? Is it being put to good use? Second, are countries to which aid is provided being transparent with their use of those resources? This may entail an uncomfortable and in-depth look we have long ignored, but I believe it will be necessary to minimize the impact that years of corruption have had on needy populaces. No one side should unfairly influence the other. And third, and quite possibly the most important evaluation, are our friends and allies conducting themselves in ways that promote personal freedom among their citizenry? That starts with us, ladies and gentlemen. Are we doing everything we can in order to promote equality? Or, are we sowing the seeds of dissension by pitting our peoples against one another?"

The murmurs were louder now. The Iraqi prime minister was stone faced. The North Korean Ambassador looked bored. Zimmer saw the Russians smiling and he returned their smiles.

"In exchange for this honest dialogue, I pledge to do everything in my power to uproot traces of corruption and bribery linked to American involvement with foreign powers. This is a two-way street, and in the coming weeks, I hope to have some very frank discussions with many of you. Everything is on the table, but at the end of the day, I hope that we can see past our differences, put aside our own egos and self interests, and instead lead by example for the citizens we represent."

The room was quiet now. Zimmer wondered what they were thinking. He urgently wanted them to think. He wanted them a bit off balance. He wanted things to change. He was done being deceived. It was time to bring the skeletons into the light.

After once again giving his thanks, he left the stage, and the voices of international representatives rose in deafening discussion. He ignored the confusion and wondered whether this "call-to-arms" for honesty, accountability, and ownership would be his undoing or end up becoming his legacy. Either way, it would be dealt with soon. He felt it was more advantageous to look into the flames than lurk in the shadows.

When he arrived at the exit, Bob Lundgren was waiting.

His face was pale, eyes wide. He looked like he was about to faint. Zimmer had never seen him so unsettled.

"Mr. President, I don't know..."

Zimmer patted him on the shoulder again and said, "Don't worry, Bob, we'll work through it."

And then he was whisked away by his Secret Service detail, leaving Lundgren open-mouthed at the door.

HAIFA, ISRAEL

August 26th, 8:11pm

C ol. Osman gritted his teeth and crushed the soda can in his hand.

"Yes, sir. I will find him," he replied, wincing at the curt retort on the other end. The call ended abruptly. He was dismissed as if he he were a lowly lieutenant.

Two days and still no word. Dr. Nahas was his responsibility. He'd been tasked to see to the scientist's well-being, and for almost a year he'd done just that. Now Nahas was gone and the two agents who'd been assigned to protect him were dead. Their bodies had been found in the classroom next door to Nahas's laboratory. The knowledge that the experienced team was taken by surprise and strangled, all in a fairly public location, led Osman to believe they were dealing with professionals. The mere fact that someone had known the top-secret location of the undercover security team made the veteran tremble with rage.

Obviously, there was a leak. Although Dr. Nahas was clueless as to what he was working on, it was now apparent someone else had that knowledge. Ergo, it was imperative to find Dr. Nahas ASAP.

Osman had ordered increased scrutiny at every border crossing and airport. Without Nahas and his tinkering, their operation might be set back months, if not a full year. Osman's superiors would not be happy should that come to pass. They had the schematics and research stored, but the final product was still in Nahas's head. In their last conversation, the inventor had promised Osman a completed prototype in two days.

The timing of Nahas's disappearance nagged at the suspicious soldier-turned-intelligence officer. His people had already tapped the phones of the doctor's family, but it was almost immediately obvious that they hadn't seen Nahas in some time. Osman remembered reading somewhere in the man's file that he had the tendency to work like a hermit for months. No wonder he hadn't married. Who would marry a man like that?

Osman had three marriages under his belt and the pelts of three divorces on his back. At least he'd found time for that.

He debated sending one of his underlings out for a cigar. He'd picked up the habit on a cross-training exercise with the Americans. There was something about the pungent richness of the cigar that made his mouth water. He pushed the craving aside and yelled towards the door.

"Maya, come in here."

A moment later, a slight young woman entered the room. Her dark eyes didn't look concerned. She was used to his outbursts. They'd worked together for close to two years. He'd stolen Maya Eilenberg from her former post within the Israeli Defense Force, where they'd had her manning a computer and plotting points on a map. Some idiot, no *idiots*, had failed to recognize her skill set. Osman could see she had untapped potential.

After he'd lost his former intelligence analyst to a corporation that paid him five times the salary Osman could offer, a brief search had unearthed Maya.

She was barely thirty and, to the casual observer, she seemed meek and unassuming. Osman had been delighted to find a sharp mind and biting tongue under that innocent facade. She could take it as well as she could dish it out. Osman liked that in a woman. His second wife was testament to that.

"Are they upset?" Maya asked, referring to the phone call.

Osman shrugged.

"What did you tell them?"

"That we would find him," Osman replied, tossing the crushed soda can in the waste basket.

"About that..."

Osman made a "Give it to me" gesture.

"No signs of Nahas," she reported. "Nothing has been reported at the airports, border crossings or ports."

"That doesn't mean he didn't leave in a box."

Maya nodded.

"...and the leak?" Osman asked.

"It wasn't us," Maya said.

"Are you sure?"

"You and I are the only ones here that know the entirety of the operation. I didn't tell anyone. Did you?"

Osman snorted. That's why he liked Maya. Who else would talk to him with such impertinence?

"What about the others?"

"It's possible, but we've been careful to tell others only what was needed. Even the two at the school thought Nahas was just another VIP."

It was true. They'd been careful. With an operation this sensitive, every aspect had been compartmentalized. Although he was no longer in uniform, Osman took his patriotic duty to his country as a sacred vow. He would personally kill anyone who got in the way of that duty.

"Okay. Keep looking. I have some friends I should talk to."

Maya nodded and went back to her office. Osman tried not to look at her rear as she left.

AN HOUR LATER, COL. OSMAN PULLED UP TO THE SECURITY camera just outside the metal gate of a three-story residence. He looked directly at the camera and a moment later the gate buzzed and shuddered to life.

His host, not quite sixty years old, awaited him at the front door wearing a look of amusement. She was still beautiful and Osman couldn't help but smile as he mounted the steps.

"Should I make drinks?" the lithe woman asked.

"I don't have time," Osman answered, reminding himself this was a business visit.

The woman shrugged and said, "Tell me you haven't changed, Ozzy. When we were married you never sat down for a chat without a cocktail."

"Fine, one drink," he huffed. Twenty years later, he still couldn't say no to the woman. If it had been up to him, they never would have gotten divorced. But at the time she had wanted children and he aspired to make general.

Neither of their wishes transpired, and they'd gone their separate ways. Well, at least personally. Hannah Krygier had gone on to enjoy much success as a force behind the Israeli political scenes. Over the years they'd kept in touch and they had swapped favors on several occasions. As a close advisor to two of the last three prime ministers, in addition to a select handful of Israeli's inner circle, Hannah was a well-placed source for Osman's periodic use. It was good to know people in high places but, although Osman got things done in the intelligence realm, his gruff demeanor precluded him from direct dealings with politicians.

Hannah was the polar opposite of Osman. She had the patience and deadly accuracy of a viper. If she wanted your career over, she could make it happen. But, on the surface, Hannah Krygier was gracious and polite.

Osman grinned as he followed her into her spacious living room. If he weren't so set in his ways and she so stubborn in hers they might still be together. She was still the most beautiful woman he had ever been with and some part of him still loved her.

She made them drinks as he sat down and admired her paintings. Hannah had always had that gift of selecting awe-inspiring paintings. He still had the ones she'd given him each year as birthday gifts. The swirls of color fascinated him almost as much as the slender curves of her tenderly aging body.

"What should we drink to?" she asked, handing him a glass full of something dark. Whiskey. She'd always liked whiskey.

"To us," Osman said, raising his glass.

Her eyebrows arched but she clinked her glass against his and they both took healthy sips.

"So, what did you really want to see me about?" Hannah asked, swirling her drink with an index finger.

"We lost Nahas."

Hannah's eyes narrowed. Osman took another healthy sip of whiskey.

"What do you mean you *lost* him?"

Osman told her about the kidnapping including the details about the two dead agents.

"Do you have any leads?" she asked.

"Not yet."

Hannah frowned.

"I brought you into this, Ozzy."

"I know and I'm grateful."

And he was. Due to Hannah's connections, she was able to set him up in a new private role as a government contractor. Were it not for Hannah's help, where would he be now?

He watched as Hannah digested the news. Osman knew what she was thinking. Word would get back to her contacts and, while her career might not be tarnished, it would look bad. Hannah did not like looking bad or inept in front of her peers.

"I don't have to tell you how important this is. If the Americans find out..."

"I know. I saw Zimmer's address," Osman said, now taking a gulp of his drink.

"How did this happen?" Hannah pressed.

"That is why I am here, Hannah. There has to be a leak."

"Have you checked your people?"

"Yes, of course. No one knew the details except for Maya and myself."

Hannah knew Maya and had gone to school with her father. There was no point asking if she was the leak. They were like family.

"So what are you saying?"

"Don't you see? The leak has to be at the government level," Osman said.

Hannah tapped her glass with her ring finger, the tinging the only sound in the room for close to a minute.

"Have you brought this to the attention of your contact?" Hannah asked, referring to the government official tasked with overseeing Osman's team.

"I wanted to tell you first. I thought you might have better ways of investigating it."

Hannah grunted.

"I'll talk to Shin Bet and see what information they can uncover."

Shin Bet, also known as the Israeli Security Agency, was the equivalent of the American FBI.

"Is that wise?"

"My friend knows how to be discreet."

Osman could tell that Hannah's mind was already running through contingencies, planning on who needed to know, and where the damage control might take them.

"What would you like me to do?" he asked.

"Do everything you can to locate Nahas. I'll let you know what I find."

He left his unfinished drink on the table and nodded his goodbye. Hannah was already on the phone, no doubt ruining some poor underling's night. Osman smiled as he returned to his car. It was always a pleasure seeing Hannah, even if during a crisis.

He was so focused on the image of her well-toned body, he never saw the blade that plunged into the back of his neck. Osman fell to his knees, the searing pain blinding him. He felt a brief relief when the blade was pulled out, releasing its grasp. He slipped down further, gurgling blood, coming to rest on his back. His body seized, and his cough sounded distant, like it came from someone else. The last thing he saw, as the edges of his vision collapsed, was a shadow opening Hannah's front door.

THE WHITE HOUSE

August 27th, 9:39am

All night, the switchboard had been flooded by calls from ambassadors, prime ministers, presidents, and generals. They all sought the same answer - what did President Zimmer's speech mean?

"Are you still sending tanks?" the Ukrainian ambassador asked.

"Will we be able to pay our soldiers?" the Afghani president asked.

"Can we still get help with our drilling efforts?" the trade envoy from Kenya asked.

The answer was always the same. "Everything stays the same until we've had a chance to do a thorough analysis. We will be in touch."

The White House staff cast glances at the Oval Office as they walked by, worry stamped on their harried features. What had the president done?

President Zimmer didn't take one phone call. He delegated that task to his well-trained team. The Chairman of the Joint Chiefs of Staff fielded the military calls. The director of the CIA dealt with his fellow intelligence chiefs. Even the vice president chipped in.

Through it all, Zimmer waited. Every hour, Bob Lundgren would enter his office and give him a rundown of the latest information and queries.

"The Saudis want assurances and the Iraqis won't shut up," he'd say. Or, "Ghana wants to know if you're still visiting next month, and South Korea needs to know about the new trade deal."

Lundgren looked like he'd aged a decade during the last twenty-four hours. His tie was askew and he'd tossed aside his suit coat hours ago. His hair wasn't much better, and Zimmer had to tell Lundgren that he had the remnants of his breakfast on his lower lip. Without a thought, the press secretary wiped it away with the back of his hand.

"I really wish you'd given me a heads-up on this, Brandon. The media is having a field day. CNN just reported that you might have lost it. Rumor is you're mentally unstable."

Zimmer's smile slipped.

"And why would they say that?" he asked curtly.

Lundgren answered without looking up from his phone, typing away furiously like he always did.

"I don't know. They said something about losing Haden, that maybe his death triggered..."

Zimmer slammed his palm on his desk, causing Lundgren to drop his phone. His mouth was half open as he tried to remember what he'd just said and then the light bulb went off.

"Look, I'm not saying *I* think that, but they think it's a little more than strange that you haven't selected a new Chief of Staff yet, that's all."

No one, except Cal's team and the president's closest advisors, knew how Travis Haden had actually died. The official story was that he'd been buried in an avalanche out west while skiing.

Zimmer controlled his breathing. It wasn't Lundgren's fault; he was just doing his job. Zimmer's speech had caused the world to turn its attention back to the White House. This was his fight.

Even so, his voice came out ice cold. "You make sure you tell anyone who brings up either my mental state or my lack of a Chief of Staff again that I'm more than happy to provide an official statement."

"You don't have to..."

"No, Bob, it seems that I do." His voice warmed. "Now look. Our team is doing great. You're doing great. Things will settle down in a couple days and when it does we'll have a much clearer picture of what we're dealing with."

Lundgren looked like he wanted to say something. For once, he didn't talk out of turn but Zimmer gestured for him to speak.

"Maybe if you gave me a hint about your plan and your goals, we could get ahead of the media cycle and spin it to our advantage."

Zimmer shook his head. That was exactly why Lundgren would never know anything but exactly what Zimmer wanted him to know.

"I'm done spinning, Bob. If you need clarification, go back and re-watch the speech. I meant what I said. I'm done financing allies, who, in turn, stab us in the back. I'm tired of it, and the American people are tired of it."

Lundgren looked like he was going to roll his eyes but thought better of it.

"I'm not saying you're not right, but come on. It's *always* been this way. We pay someone to get what we want. Sure there's some corruption behind the scenes but how the hell can we stop that?"

"Just like I said, Bob. Now, unless you have anything else..."

Lundgren shook his head and picked the phone up from the floor.

"I'll be back in an hour," he said, already heading for the door.

"Thanks, Bob. I meant what I said. The team is doing great."

Lundgren nodded absently as he went on his way.

The president turned back to his computer and scrolled through more of the day's headlines.

Zimmer Throws Down The Gauntlet

"No More Soup For You!" says Zimmer

Zimmer: The Isolationist?

He shook his head with a mix of frustration and despair. He closed the web browser. He had learned early on during his presidency that in order to get things done he had to look past the constant news stream. However, with social media an ever-present source of information, it was hard to look away.

It was also quite impossible to ignore the 700-point dip on Wall Street and the riots in Greece. The world economy felt like it was teetering on the verge of collapse. He had just thrown more into the mix. Time would tell which way it would tip. It was possible the system would self-correct instead of crumbling like a demolished building. Time would tell.

More than the headlines, Zimmer thought about what he *wasn't* hearing. Sure there were the complaints and the concerns. However, there were certain parties who hadn't reached out to the White House. The Russians were obviously digesting the new information and most likely plotting or maneuvering a way to take advantage of the situation. Zimmer wouldn't be surprised to hear that Iran was doubling down in the West Bank in the coming days. Of greater concern was that some of their closest allies hadn't reached out either in solidarity or to voice their dissention.

He made a note to ask the CIA and the NSA about these concerns. He'd felt it coming, like a tsunami building over the horizon. The speech at the U.N. had been something he and Travis had talked about for months. For some reason, he'd felt compelled to pull that trigger. Maybe it would help and maybe it would hurt. It was too soon to know.

Deep in his gut something told Zimmer that the speech might bring about something else entirely and that the most important outcome was it just might predict the oncoming storm.

THE JEFFERSON GROUP HEADQUARTERS

Charlottesville, Virginia

AUGUST 27TH, 11:30AM

The steady hum of computer fans and spinning drives whirred around Neil Patel like an orchestra. As the maestro of the song, Neil controlled the impressive array of monitors and the infinite processes with a detached ease. This was his home, his domain.

Today was his catch-up day. As the man behind every piece of technology utilized by The Jefferson Group, it was Neil's job to ensure everything was functioning properly. This was no small task, and a tedious bore that would normally rest on the shoulders of a team of IT specialists. However, the periodic checks were essential for the proper running of the company's consultancy tasks.

There were, of course, the clients to keep track of and the projects requiring completion. But, it was the other side of The Jefferson Group that provided the majority of the horse-power from Neil's ever-evolving collection of tech toys and computer advancements.

On paper, The Jefferson Group advertised itself to the

public as a private consultancy firm offering services to diverse industries like security and education. Their clients included large corporations like Boeing and institutions like the University of Virginia, on whose grounds The Jefferson Group's headquarters now resided. The company's CEO was Jonas Layton, a young self-made billionaire, known as "The Fortuneteller" by most of the who's-who of the corporate elite. Jonas was The Jefferson Group's public face, and he was also responsible for running the day-to-day operations of the company.

Hidden far from the eyes of the public lay the real guts of The Jefferson Group. The covert team answered only to one man - President Brandon Zimmer. In short, the men of The Jefferson Group were an elite direct action force residing within the president's back pocket, ready to deploy at any given moment.

But for the past few months they'd lain idle waiting for their leader to return. Cal Stokes was such a man that men like Neil Patel, Dr. Alvin Higgins (former CIA lead interrogator), and a select group of operators had left their former home (Stokes Security International (SSI)) for him. Now Cal was MIA, and the president hadn't called upon their services. The men of The Jefferson Group (TJG) spoke of it often, wondering whether Cal would return as their fearless leader. They also pondered if President Zimmer had lost his nerve after Travis Haden's death.

Because, beneath the intrigue and the training, behind the professionalism and the bloodshed, these men were friends. They were brothers, and each one felt the same kinship for their president. He had sacrificed for them as they'd fought missions for him.

Currently, they were without not only their leader, but also they did not have any missions to conduct. That didn't mean they didn't stay busy. The warriors among them trained at Camp Cavalier, the SSI campus just down the road from UVA. Neil stayed occupied as he hacked and sifted through the endless chatter online. Jonas secured more clients, while Dr. Higgins gave talks up and down the east coast. This way they kept their skills sharpened and their minds focused during this rare operational sabbatical. They felt the itch to do something more, yet they had the patience to wait it out to provide Cal time to heal.

With weekly updates from Daniel, at least they knew Cal was okay. Each of them, save Jonas, had been to war and had experienced loss. More importantly, they'd all known and respected Travis. They felt his absence keenly, and his name often came up in toasts.

As the steel-reinforced door swung open, an alert pinged on Neil's computer screen. Master Sergeant Willy Trent, a nearly seven-foot tall, ebony-skinned Marine strolled into the room, closely followed by Gaucho, a short stocky Hispanic operator almost half Trent's height.

"I said I believed you," Trent was saying, "I'm sure your grandmother's enchiladas are better than mine."

"You better believe it, Top," Gaucho said, shaking his head causing his dual-braided beard to swing back and forth against his chest. "Man, just thinking about Abuelita's enchiladas makes my mouth water."

He made an exaggerated smacking sound with his lips causing Trent to laugh.

Willy Trent was a classically-trained chef in addition to his elite Marine Corps experience. The chiseled former Marine felt as comfortable tossing a 300-pound thug over his shoulder as he did making Crème Brûlée.

Neil clicked the flashing dialogue box as he asked, "What are you two fighting about now?"

Trent and Gaucho were forever giving each other a hard time. It probably had something to do with the fact that they were inseparable and best friends. That led to many memorable conversations where they became the center of attention. The mismatched pair verbally sparred while the rest of The Jefferson Group howled in laughter from the fringe.

"I said something to Jonas about making enchiladas and Gaucho said that I could never make them like his grandmother," Trent answered.

"Ain't no way," Gaucho said, his head bobbing in earnest.

"Look, I already told you…"

Neil, in an attempt to get their attention, snapped his fingers. He was intently looking at his computer screen, eyes wide.

"What is it?" Trent asked, moving closer.

Neil put a finger in the air, asking his friends to wait. Finally he said, "Holy crap."

"What is it?" Trent asked again.

Neil shook his head like he couldn't believe what he'd just seen.

"I need to get this to Daniel," Neil said.

Trent and Gaucho had kept their distance, always leery about getting into Neil's personal tech space.

"What is it?" Trent asked, for a third time.

Neil pointed at the monitor and motioned for the two squabbling men to step closer. Both sets of eyes went wide.

"Holy crap," Trent and Gaucho said in unison.

"Yeah, like I said, I need to get this to Daniel."

WILD DUNES: ISLE OF PALMS, SOUTH CAROLINA

The round of golf hadn't helped. Even though the balls flew straight and the putts rarely veered, Cal barely made it through seven holes. It took a foursome of old-timers to get him moving as he'd sat in his golf cart and gazed into nothingness.

Next, he'd gone for a long walk, one of many he'd taken over the past five months. He walked around the northern point of the Isle of Palms until he reached the point where Cedar Creek fed the inlet. Then he headed back south and grabbed a cup of fruit and a bottle of water at the Wild Dunes Grand Pavilion. One especially sauced divorcée couldn't help herself and insisted on buying him a drink. Her friends saw the vacant look in his eyes and dragged her away as quickly as they could.

After tossing half the fruit cup in the trash, he continued walking past the vacation homes where families were enjoying the tail end of summer. He turned around at the pier next to Isle of Palms County Park and headed home.

When he got there, an unexpected guest was waiting on the steps.

Daniel Briggs rose and gave Cal a nod.

"Hey," Cal said. He knew Daniel had been around; he'd developed a sixth sense regarding the sniper's presence.

"I'm sorry to surprise you like this," Daniel said.

Cal shrugged like it didn't matter. Nothing really mattered to him anymore.

"How've you been?" Cal asked. It was nice to see his friend again. He hadn't realized how much he had missed him until Daniel spoke.

"Good. I've got something for you."

"Wanna come inside?"

"Sure."

Cal led the way, locking the door after Daniel entered. Neither man said a word as they climbed the stairs to the third floor. Someone had left a pile of fruit on the counter, probably the maid.

"You want anything to drink?" Cal asked.

"No, thanks."

Cal went to the pantry, grabbed a bottle of water and

chugged it. It was then he noticed Daniel was holding a single folded sheet of paper.

"What's that?" Cal asked.

"Neil found it when he was doing some clean-up work for SSI. He says none of their staff found it because SSI isn't doing much operational work anymore."

Cal was confused. He knew Neil still did a fair share of work for SSI, and he still held the role of Chief Technology Officer, but he had no idea what Daniel was talking about.

"It's a Last Letter," Daniel said, addressing the unspoken question.

The dim bulb in the back of Cal's head switched on. SSI had a small digital database that housed letters written by operators to their loved ones prior to deploying. They called them "Last Letters" and they were typically notes to wives, girlfriends or their children. The letters were never seen unless the operator was killed in action. That hadn't happened in some time since before Cal's departure from his father's company.

"I don't understand," Cal said. "Who's it from?"

There was something in Daniel's eyes, something that engaged Cal's fight-or-flight response. He wanted to run.

"It's from Travis."

A gunshot to his sternum couldn't have had the same impact as those words. Cal's chest seized and his knees threatened to buckle. Somehow, though his breath wouldn't come. He reached for the paper and unfolded it. It was a digital scan of a handwritten note and he recognized Travis's handwriting immediately. He took a breath.

Cal,

I haven't written one of these in a while. Feels strange, but why not?

I know we don't like to talk about stuff like this a lot, but I wanted to tell you something. I'm proud of you, Cal. You may be a dumb grunt, but you're the best man I've ever known. No shit. There's a reason guys like Daniel and Top run after you without thinking. Hell, I'm about to do the same thing, run to your bugle call.

You've got something man, something I admit I don't even have. You get it. You just get it. You inspire confidence and you lead like few men I've ever known. Your dad would be proud, Cal, really proud.

But there's one thing, and this is a tough one. Maybe I'll tell you if this letter isn't necessary, and then again maybe I won't.

I know how personally you take things. It's one of the things that makes you a phenomenal leader. It's only natural. You're passionate, you're driven, and you care. You love your men more than you love yourself.

But, I've got a secret to tell you, Cal. Your men know what they're getting into. They know the risks; we all do. Sometimes shit happens. Sometimes people die and we wonder why. Don't. Don't wonder why. It just is.

Do me a favor, Cuz. If I go before you do, throw me the biggest fucking party you can. Get drunk, propose to that pretty girl of yours and remember what a bad-ass I was.
(I was pretty amazing).

We're about to land and I'll see you in a minute, so it's time to wrap this up. Hopefully this note will find its way to the trash bin when we get done, but if it doesn't, know that I love you, that I'm proud of you, and that I'll see you again, but hopefully not too soon.

Semper Fi, Jarhead, and Hooyah, Cuz,
Trav

Cal looked up from the letter, his eyes stinging from the tears. Daniel waited, wearing the same patient look he always had whether before entering harm's way or while they were talking over dinner.

Cal sniffed and wiped his eyes on his arm.

"How did you get through it?" Cal asked. He didn't have to explain what he was talking about. Daniel knew his friend was talking about the pain of loss.

"One step at a time...and a lot of Jack Daniels."

Cal chuckled and wiped his eyes again.

"Can you do me a favor?" he asked.

Daniel nodded.

Cal smiled and said through a cracking voice, "Call the boys and tell them to get down here. I've got a big fucking party to throw."

The old-fashioned metal lettering, *The Ludlow Report,* on the wall flickered, now illuminated for the camera. It also provided a cue to the talk show's host that one minute remained before they went live. He was excited about today's segment for two reasons. First, he was finally filling in for Damon Ludlow, the regular host, who was currently cruising the Caribbean with his fourth wife. Second, and of more significance, he had the opportunity to talk about the topic that had the world aflutter - President Brandon Zimmer's address at the U.N.

"Thirty seconds," announced the producer, pointing directly at the host, Ken Wick, who had only missed his cue once but the producer would never let him forget it. Instead of flipping the man off, he flashed a pearly smile before turning his undivided attention to his guests.

He counted down the seconds in his head and tried not to hold his breath. Before he knew it, the red light on the lead camera came on and *The Ludlow Report*'s theme music played overhead. He looked directly into the camera and began speaking.

"Good evening, America, and welcome to *The Ludlow Report*. I am your host, Ken Wick." He paused allowing the last syllable to hang in the air before continuing, "Tonight, I'm filling in for Damon Ludlow, currently on vacation. Sitting across from me are tonight's guests. Van Bloodgood is a former analyst for the Central Intelligence Agency, and currently the principal at a Boston-based think tank specializing in international policy. Thank you for joining us, Mr. Bloodgood."

"Thank you for having me, Mr. Wick," Bloodgood replied with a nod of his massive head.

"And tonight's second esteemed guest is the former U.S. Ambassador to Denmark and current professor of international relations at Princeton, Ambassador Engelbert Wheatley. Thank you for joining us, Ambassador."

"It is my pleasure, Ken."

Ken Wick noticed that the ambassador's smile was even whiter than his own. He'd selected the two men himself and the differences couldn't have been more obvious. While Ambassador Wheatley looked like an ambassador, tall and stately, Van Bloodgood looked like a bull mastiff, large and imposing. Even his name sounded ominous. Wick was sure the audience would eat that up.

"Now gentlemen, we don't have a lot of time, so I'd like to get right to it. I, along with the rest of the world, would love to know your thoughts on President Zimmer's recent remarks at the United Nations."

The guests looked at one another and with a nod of his head the former CIA analyst deferred to the ambassador.

Wheatley began. "Now, Ken, while I admire the president's courage, I am not sure I agree with the way he is executing his agenda."

"Could you elaborate, Ambassador?"

Wheatley nodded, taking a moment of thoughtful

contemplation before answering. Wick knew this was all for show. It was a well-known fact that the Ambassador loved being in the spotlight.

"In my time with the State Department and during my tenure as ambassador, I couldn't tell you how many times I witnessed our allies blatantly abusing the aid we provided. Now, while it may sound noble that the president wants to wipe the slate clean and dispose of every nefarious character he can, I think it is naive to say that is even possible."

"But don't you think it is well within our right to examine the ways in which our aid is being used?" Wick asked.

"Of course, but it could have been done behind closed doors like we've done for years."

Van Bloodgood shifted in his seat, his placid face swiveling to face Wheatley.

"And how do you think those policies have served us thus far, Ambassador?" Bloodgood asked, snatching the role of host from Wick.

It took every ounce of self-control for Ken not to squirm with glee. This was exactly what he wanted. A confrontation would boost ratings. Hell, it might even push the bigwigs up at corporate to let him do more hosting. As far as he was concerned, Damon Ludlow was on the way out and Ken Wick was on his way in.

Wheatley was responding, "While we may have hit a few snags along the way, I do believe that by and large our foreign policy, specifically our aid packages, hold up well under intense examination."

"And what about our supposed allies?" Bloodgood asked, his droopy eyelids never moving.

"What about them, Mr. Bloodgood?"

"Do you believe that our allies have taken advantage of their favored statuses and have, at times, turned right around and thrown our goodwill back in our face?"

Wheatley chuckled. "Yes, as I mentioned before, I have witnessed such inconveniences in my time overseas."

"And what did you do to stop those transgressions, Ambassador?"

Wheatley's face reddened for the briefest moment. Wick noticed it immediately and hoped the moron behind the camera had caught it too because the ambassador's outward congeniality quickly returned.

"As with any discrepancy I or my staff reported them through the proper channels."

"And do you believe that reporting those discrepancies helped improve the system as a whole?" Bloodgood asked. Nothing but the man's mouth and jowls moved.

"I am sure they did," Wheatley replied, returning to Wick.

"But how do you know?" Bloodgood pressed. "Can you give us one example of how the system righted itself?"

Wick saw another crack in Wheatley's demeanor. The Ambassador was staring at him like he needed to moderate the conversation. Wick obliged.

"I'm sorry, Mr. Bloodgood, our time is limited. Let's move on to the next question. This time we'll begin with you."

Bloodgood nodded. He looked almost bored.

"Mr. Bloodgood, how do you think the president should respond to the accusations leveled by fellow world leaders following his U.N. address?"

"I think he should stand his ground."

"Would you like to elaborate?"

Bloodgood leaned forward.

"I think the president's correct. If the American people knew the extent to which we've been seduced and abused by our allies, I am sure there would be quite the outcry for accountability. It is the taxpayers' dollars being abused. We give away trillions without a good system for tracking its usage. Sure, we say there are checks and balances, but in reality, sometimes we're just going on blind faith."

"Should we not have faith in our allies, Mr. Bloodgood?" Ambassador Wheatley interjected. "We are all human after all, and no system is perfect." He chuckled but Bloodgood did not return the laugh.

Instead he said, "*We are human*, Mr. Wheatley, and a government-run system is far from perfect." Wick saw Wheatley bristle but his face was turned from the live camera. "That is why we need a periodic reevaluation like the one the president has proposed."

Somehow Wheatley held back a snort. "So, you're saying that we should throw away decades, and in some cases centuries, of diplomacy just so that *you* can feel better about the system itself?"

"Not for me, Ambassador, but for the American people."

"Excuse me?"

"Like the president, I believe that the American people have to feel better about where their hard-earned dollars are being spent."

"Well, of course they do, but the time..."

"The time it takes is irrelevant. You said it yourself, the abuses are real. They will always be real. What President Zimmer has said is that if you intend to be our ally and receive the enormous benefits of an alliance with the U.S., you'd better do your best to make sure you and your citizenry are doing what you're supposed to be doing. I don't see why that's so difficult to comprehend. It is not an unfair requisite either."

This time Wheatley did laugh. "Mr. Bloodgood, I don't think you fully understand the implications of such an undertaking." Even Wick thought the ambassador sounded like a snob with that comment and he was on Wheatley's side. It was time to step in.

"Well, gentlemen, it seems that we have much more to discuss after we take a quick commercial break." He turned to the camera and said, "When we come back, our guests will give us their predictions regarding the effects of The Zimmer Doctrine."

THE WHITE HOUSE

President Zimmer sighed and turned off the television. At least he had one admirer. It seemed like the rest of the world was lining up to take pot shots at both him and his proposal. He'd spent the day calming his harried staff and making calls to legislators on both sides of the aisle. Everyone was confused and wanted to know the plan.

There was no formulated plan as of yet. He was still figuring it out along the way. Hell, he didn't even know what the expected outcome would look like.

What he wouldn't give to have Travis there. Together, they would've figured it out. But he had faith that the answer would come soon. It might come in the natural course of their investigations. The answer could come from one of his advisors or maybe a fellow head of state. Maybe through playing damage control a path would form to improve the system. Either way, it was too late to go back now.

He tossed the remote on the bed and pulled a T-shirt over his head. It would be good to get away. Maybe with a little space his team could get the bipartisan commission formed.

Tonight he had a party to go to, and the helicopter was awaiting his departure. Nothing in the world would prevent him from attending this momentous occasion to celebrate Travis's life.

UNKNOWN LOCATION

August 27th, 8:22pm

"Is the cargo hold ready?"

"Yes, Captain," replied the man wearing a pair of coveralls with light streaks of grease on his pant legs. Normally, the captain would have told the crewman to change his clothing. After all, he ran a respectable vessel but his mind was consumed with other problems.

"And you're sure the new railing system can support the weight?"

"The final test showed no excess pressure, Captain. The railing could carry twice the weight, if needed."

The captain suppressed a frown. Things were going too quickly. His men should've had at least another month of preparations before going operational. But the powers that be had made their decision known in no uncertain terms that now was the time.

"Very well," the captain said, smoothing back his black hair. "Commence with the loading."

The crewman nodded and left the bridge. The captain followed two minutes later after dispatching a brief radio transmission to a local relay station. The message was innocuous enough so as to never raise an alarm. It was all part of the plan. In order to stay concealed from the prying eyes of the Americans, they had to play it safe. Playing it safe meant handling things the old way, using messengers and seemingly archaic technology.

The captain had first learned how to use a shortwave radio as a child. It was what first led him to the navy and now to his current position. He smiled at the memory and marveled at the utility and reliability of such simple tools. The Americans would never suspect. They'd been too busy chasing down Islamists since 9/11 and now their president had incurred the world's wrath for his remarks at the United Nations.

The captain chuckled and grabbed his hat from the helm. He stroked the gold ropes on the bill for a moment and once more ran through his mission. His superiors called it a bullet-proof plan. As far as he was concerned, there was no such thing as a bulletproof plan. Add a detail and the probability of defeat multiplied. Add one hundred and your luck would inevitably turn.

He tried to ignore his ever-present pessimism and tried to focus on the goal. He could go down in history for this and nobody would even know. A handful of men and women would give him and his men medals, heralding them heroes, but that wasn't what was important. The captain wanted one thing and that was for his country to regain its rightful place on the world stage. If he was just another cog in the plan, so be it. But if it meant being on the leading edge and laying the groundwork for what could secure his country's future for years to come, he would die a happy man.

The captain slipped on his white cap and checked his reflection in the window. After stroking his mustache twice, he made his way aft.

At EXACTLY 9 PM, A SEMI PULLING A FLATBED TRAILER stopped one hundred feet from the end of the pier. Within minutes, straps were undone; hooks and clamps were secured to the large package. One minute later, the pier's crane lifted the package off of the bed. Using hand signals and the occasional curse, the ship's crew directed the operator's expert handling of the crane.

The parcel was lowered into the cargo hold where it was then mounted to its custom frame. Five minutes later, the man in the greasy overalls gave a thumbs-up, and the crane withdrew the hook from the vessel.

Now there was a frenzy of activity as the rest of the crew prepared to get underway. The captain watched it all from the aft helo deck.

"Is there anything else you require?" asked the man standing to his right. He wore a suit and a heavy overcoat, despite the mild weather. They'd been both friends and compatriots for almost thirty years.

"Get me as many of these as you can," the captain said.

"Do you mean the boat or the cargo?" his friend asked, a note of humor in his voice.

"You know how I feel about your calling this vessel a boat." It was the same conversation they'd had since rooming together in boarding school. The captain's friend was not a navy man, had never served in the military, and pretended not to know a thing about its capabilities. But he did and only feigned ignorance to annoy the captain.

"Would you still be cross with me if I told you that I smuggled a case of Scotch aboard?"

The captain's mouth watered. He'd allow himself a nip or two once they made their way far from the coast. The beauty under his feet could practically get to the other side of the world by herself but he was still the captain.

"You're sure you won't come with us?" the captain asked with a wry grin.

His friend moaned, grabbing his stomach. "The last time I took you up on that offer I lost half a bottle of twenty-year aged Scotch overboard."

The captain chuckled. "You're lucky it was raining or I would have made you clean it up."

His friend shrugged and directed his attention back to the busy crew.

"We are doing the right thing, you know."

The captain nodded. Initially, he had not thought highly of the plan. It had seemed like suicide on so many levels. But when his friend had explained the breadth of what he'd concocted, it only took the captain a day to swear his allegiance.

"You can stop trying to convince me," the captain said. "Just make sure the rest of them do what is necessary for a successful outcome."

"They know what to do."

His friend was right. He was only one of many who'd been chosen for service. Military training aside, it was what they'd done as civilians while still maintaining their ties to their homeland. They had the experience, including the skill of not drawing unnecessary attention to themselves, acting like chameleons. The captain told himself not to worry, all would be well.

"Fair winds, Captain," his friend said, holding out his hand.

"And following seas," the captain answered, grasping the extended hand. Both men nodded to one another. There was nothing left to say. Without another word, his friend descended the ladder to the main deck below.

The captain turned from the railing and headed towards the bridge. In fifteen minutes they would be pulling away from the pier. After that it was a straight shot across the Atlantic. He'd made the trip countless times before, but never before had he been carrying the message he now held below deck.

* * *

TWENTY-SEVEN OTHER VESSELS LEFT THEIR RESPECTIVE ports within the next six hours. Their crews were loyal and their objectives clear. With destinations scattered across the globe, this would be the first of many trips if all went according to plan.

Their country had suffered at the hands of its enemies and allies alike. Their once-proud citizenry now stood on the second tier of the world stage, and the men on the crews of the twenty-eight vessels yearned to fight their way back to the top.

And so they left their moorings under the cover of darkness, their destinations known by the captains alone. The vessels would travel as they had in their previous journeys, taking circuitous routes and lazy meandering loops along paradise coasts. They had time, which they would use to their advantage.

WILD DUNES

Isle of Palms, South Carolina

T he beach bonfire threw its flames into the moonlit sky as if daring the waning orb to shine brighter. Country music thumped from a large Bluetooth speaker. Just what Travis would've wanted; country music and Jack Daniels.

While the music played, the liquor flowed freely as the twenty-odd guests chatted and told stories about Travis, the former CEO of SSI, who had been their boss and, more importantly, their friend.

"Remember that time Travis told Top that he was getting recalled to the Corps? Man, I wish I'd had a camera to capture that look on your face," Gaucho said, howling at the memory and pointing a stubby finger at his best friend.

Most of them were there now. Jonas Layton and Dr. Higgins had arrived via the company jet flown by the brothers, Jim and Johnny Powers, along with their fellow pilot, Benny Fletcher, who was a former Army Apache ace. The last three men hadn't known Travis well, but they laughed right along with the others. It was hard not to laugh when Gaucho and Trent were storytelling.

"You remember when Travis convinced us to go on that cold weather op in Alaska?" Trent said, eliciting a pained look from Gaucho. "I've never seen Gaucho so miserable."

"Don't remind me, man," Gaucho answered, taking a healthy swig of his drink as if it would erase the memory. "I still can't feel the tips of my big toes."

Through it all Cal felt like he was on the verge of tears, but happy tears. Tears shed for a soul lost, but one that would never be forgotten. During the past five months he had been so engrossed in his own pain that he'd never once considered the pain felt by his friends. As he watched them laugh and drink, arms often draped across each other's shoulders and exchanging playful jabs between shots, Cal's mind refocused. It was like coming out of an impenetrable fog. It was more like an unseen enemy had dropped the world's largest and densest smoke grenade. The smoke had hurt him at first, blinded him and then muted his senses. But now the smoke was clearing and his senses were returning. Due to Travis's letter and, more importantly, the presence of his friends, Cal felt he was beginning to return to his former self.

"It's good to see them," Daniel said, his voice low so only Cal could hear.

Cal nodded. He felt ashamed for keeping Daniel from the others. Ever since his outburst at Travis's funeral, Daniel had been staying close and watching over Cal from a distance.

"Hey, I'm sorry that you had to come down here and..."

Daniel's smile and the subtle shake of his head cut off the rest of Cal's apology. Cal knew that Daniel understood what he'd gone through and what he was still going through. The stubborn Marine wasn't foolish enough to think that this was the end of it. His pain might subside, but it would never completely go away. He just had to learn to live with it, to channel the pain in productive ways that would help make a difference in the world. After all, that's what Travis would want.

"It's too bad you don't drink," Cal said, gesturing to the folding table that held handles of Jack Daniels and Famous Grouse, a toast to the old days at SSI. In addition, there was water and an ice bucket.

"I'm sure you guys can polish that off."

Cal grinned, savoring the warmth in his chest and the lightness that seemed to increase with every passing minute. The burdensome weight was lifting; he could feel it.

Marjorie Haines, the current CEO of SSI, was the next to arrive. She was accompanied by the burly form of Todd Dunn, SSI's head of security. Going back a couple of years, she and Travis had been an item. Lost in a sea of his own despair, Cal had forgotten to reach out to Marge. He could see that she was trying to keep it together, and he wondered how she had coped with Travis's tragic death.

He made his way to her, nodding a greeting to Dunn, a man of few words.

"Thanks for coming," Cal said.

"We wouldn't miss it," Marge answered. Her tough facade that had helped to give her the nickname,"The Hammer," slipped and Cal saw the anguish in her eyes.

"Marge, I'm so sorry."

She nodded. One tear dropped from her eye, quickly followed by more. Cal pulled her into a tight embrace and she sobbed quietly. If the others noticed, they didn't let on. With the music and sounds of laughter in the background, Cal held his old friend as the pain flowed from her.

Marge looked up, her wet eyes clearing.

"I'm sorry, too."

Cal smiled warmly and said. "Come on. We've both shed our tears. Now it's time to drink."

Marge returned the smile and dabbed at her eyes with a tissue Todd Dunn produced from his coat pocket.

"Let me guess, Travis's idea?" she said, pointing to the rows of dark liquid.

"You think *I* would throw a party like this?" Cal asked with amusement.

Marge slapped his arm playfully and went to visit with the others. Cal watched as Trent gave her his trademark bear hug and the others extended handshakes. She was one of them, even if they were no longer part of the same organization.

"How's she been?" Cal asked Dunn, who let his boss make the rounds.

"Stays busy mostly."

"And you?"

At one time, Dunn had been Travis's bodyguard, confidante, and loyal friend - similar to the relationship between Cal and Daniel.

"I miss him," Dunn said. Cal knew it was probably the only emotional overture he'd get from the former Army Ranger. If you looked up the word stoic in the dictionary there was a ninety percent chance you would see Todd Dunn's image there.

"Why don't you grab a drink? Snake Eyes has the watch," Cal said, pointing to ever-vigilant Daniel.

Dunn nodded, moving into the firelight, shaking hands with his former companions, once more part of the crew.

A few minutes later, two large figures emerged from the darkness. Cal tensed for a moment but Daniel waved a hand in acknowledgment. One of the men waved back and, after a quick scan of the area, disappeared back into the shadows from whence they had come. Cal was about to ask Daniel what was going on when President Brandon Zimmer, dressed in casual khaki shorts and a polo shirt, stepped into the firelight.

This time the voices around the fire fell silent as Brandon made a beeline for Cal. The Zac Brown band still strummed in the background, their smooth melody warding off the stillness.

"I didn't know you were coming," Cal said when Brandon neared.

"I wouldn't miss it," Brandon replied and Cal knew he meant it.

The two men stood there for an awkward moment, Cal remembering the scene he had made after the funeral in front of the president and his team. That had been the last time he'd seen the president..

"I'm sorry about, well you know, the thing at Trav's funeral," Cal offered.

"Don't worry about it."

Another pause. Neither knew quite what to say. They were like brothers whose bond had been split by an accident, a tragic loss. This time the silence was broken when Trent stomped up and wrapped a muscled arm first around Brandon and then around Cal.

"If you two ladies are done making up, I think there's a little booze we need to drink," Trent said, evoking a chuckle from both men. "You think I'm kidding, but Doc Higgins is giving me a run for my money."

"Hold on, Top," Brandon said, "I stopped and picked up a friend along the way."

Cal's face scrunched in confusion and then he turned as the president motioned back the way he'd arrived. There, standing in the flickering light with her hair braided to one side the way he liked it and wearing a simple striped sundress was Diane Mayer. They made eye contact and Cal felt his heart pounding in his throat, making it impossible to speak. Again came the pang of regret. He hadn't called her after the funeral. The others had probably kept her apprised of his location but she'd never pressed.

At one point, months ago, this beautiful woman had been the force that had grounded the Marine. Her intellect intrigued him, her humor enthralled him, and her voice covered him like a salve.

Instead of allowing Diane to help him deal with his grief, Cal had repaid her love by running away, just as he had shunned his team. He'd hidden from the world, from his sorrow, and from her. He didn't know what to say. What do you say to a person after you leave them for months with no explanation, no word?

He didn't know and yet he went to her, pulled once again by the inexplicable force that attracts two soul-entwined beings.

"Hi," he said, looking into her eyes and then glancing at the sand at his feet.

"Hi," she answered. He felt the hesitation. He'd *hurt* her; he'd *left* her. He, not anyone else.

Cal pushed the guilt away and focused on Travis's words. *Sometimes shit happens*.

"I'm sorry," he said, wishing there was some way to imbue the words with magical powers that would relay the depth of his plea.

"I know," she said, in a tone much nicer than he thought he deserved. He almost wished she would slap him, throw sand in his face, or do something to repay him for his sins. But she didn't. Instead she asked, "Can you get me a drink?"

He looked up at her, and while he didn't see a look that said she would accept him back with open arms, he did see that she was trying. That was all he deserved and more than he'd ever hoped for. All the words that he'd tried to get straight in his head earlier in the day now muddled together like alphabet soup. The only thing he could say was, "Famous Grouse or Jack?"

She smiled shyly and said, "Jack please, and you better make it a double."

HAIFA, ISRAEL

August 28th, 4:47am Israel Daylight Time (IDT)

Maya Eilenberg prayed for the first rays of sunlight to come. She'd been on the run for almost twenty-four hours. Maya had seen the covert operatives following her but she had probably missed others. She couldn't be sure but they were there. It had all started with a call from her adopted aunt, Hannah Krygier, with an imminent warning.

"You must find a place to hide, Maya. Quickly."

Coming from Krygier, the message could not have been clearer. Aunt Hannah, as Maya called her, was the epitome of calm. Maya often wished that she possessed such poise.

Two hours after talking to her Aunt Hannah, she'd received a similar call, this time from a robotic-sounding voice that informed her that Colonel Osman was dead. It was imperative she come in for questioning.

When she hung up the phone her face must have paled, because the cab driver asked if she was okay. Maya nodded curtly, regained a measure of composure and ordered the driver to pull over at the next stoplight. He did and, after paying the man, Maya hit the pavement, weaving her way in and out of rush hour pedestrian traffic.

Her training kicked into high gear. From behind darkly tinted sunglasses, she began her hyper-vigilant scan of threats. It was impossible to confirm her suspicions, but she thought she had seen the same two men repeatedly. It could have been a coincidence when she saw one man buying food from a vendor and another perusing a newspaper stand. When she saw the same two men a second time, she knew it was no longer coincidental. They blended in perfectly. One was slender and dressed in casual business attire while the other wore a dusty construction uniform, carrying a yellow hardhat under his arm.

She could run. She knew how to disappear. If someone in her line of work didn't have an escape plan, they were either extremely careless or suicidal. Luckily, Col. Osman had taught her the skills needed to be an effective agent. He'd been a good boss, although a bit flirtatious at times. But while other men only saw a pretty face, Osman had seen her potential. After testing her intelligence, the army veteran had insisted Maya receive additional training as an operator, which included the use of weapons, hand-to-hand combat, and evasive maneuvers.

Not only had she excelled in her duties, but she'd been surprised to find that advanced weapons training and spy-craft fit perfectly with her unassuming demeanor. In Osman's words, she was a natural.

That didn't mean she held any illusions about taking on a man twice her size in hand-to-hand combat, but there were other ways to get the job done. Currently, she needed to utilize her evasive training to get the men off her trail.

Maya made up her mind and crossed the busy street, waving apologies to honking vehicles. She then approached the slender man who was sitting on a bench seemingly concerned only with his meal. If he was following her, he was *very* good. He didn't look up at her when she, now playing the role of a lost pedestrian, approached him.

"Excuse me, can you tell me how to get to the train station?" she asked the man while continually glancing at her watch to give him the idea she was running late for an appointment.

He looked up from his food and pointed down the street.

"Head towards the port. You can't miss it."

"Thank you," she said, already heading in the direction he'd indicated. As she crossed the next intersection, she glanced back casually and noted the man was now intently speaking on his phone. He hadn't gotten up from his seat but when Maya's gaze swiveled wide she saw the other man across the street with a cell phone pressed to his ear.

However, two minutes later she scanned the area again. Both men had disappeared. A minute later, she looked again, but there were no signs of the men. Instead of calming her nerves, the absence of the men heightened her malaise. In the direction she was going, the crowds were thinning. She had yet to locate an unoccupied taxi.

That's when it occurred to her they'd been using the surveillance cameras in order to determine her location and keep tabs on her movements. The cameras were present everywhere. In a time when bombings were common throughout Israel, authorities had made it a top priority to install surveillance along major thoroughfares and throughout all major transportation hubs. Maya bit her lip instead of cursing; she imagined Osman laughing at her stupidity.

Even as she chided herself for the rookie move, a cab crept by, the backseat empty. She banged on the trunk to get his attention. The cab stopped, and she approached the driver's side window.

"Get in," the man said, after giving her a once over.

She ignored the ogling as she slid into the backseat. When asked where she wanted to go, she told him the airport. From there she'd caught another cab back into the city. Then she headed into the hills and their residential neighborhoods. Five cabs and a long walk later, she'd arrived at her current location. She discovered a dingy flat with a crooked sign on the lawn announcing a vacancy. It was after midnight but, despite the time, she called the number on the sign.

The owner, while less than amused by the late-night call, happily met her ten minutes later, but only after she offered to pay cash for a month's rent. It turned out that the fat slob lived downstairs and even offered her a drink in his flat. If she hadn't been moving all day, she might have taken him up on the offer, if only to keep up appearances. But her body and mind were exhausted, and she'd promised the landlord that she'd buy him a bottle of wine the next day. Maya had no intention of being in the apartment for that long, but he didn't have to know that.

She'd secured the apartment door as well as she could and crumpled onto the bed. Even though she was bone tired, sleep would not come. She'd been lying in the same position staring up at the mottled ceiling as her brain spun, her senses still on high alert.

Finally, she made up her mind. She'd dumped her cell phone shortly after the robotic message but there were still pay phones scattered throughout the city. What she really wanted to do was run. With the resources she had scattered in various safety deposit boxes around town, Maya was sure she could live for at least two years.

But where would that leave her? On a beach selling trinkets until she was old and wrinkled? No, she could never do that. She wasn't even in her thirties yet. There was still too much she wanted to do. Her job with Osman was supposed to be her meal ticket, and until twenty-four hours before, it had been. Their operation wasn't just the most interesting thing she'd ever worked on, it was also highly fulfilling to her deep patriotism.

Maya believed in her country and wanted to do everything in her power to protect its future. But how could she do that if she was on the run? More importantly, who was the leak in their operation and who had killed Osman?

Like so many operators around the world, Maya Eilenberg's mind kept wandering back to the same scenario, one she did not really want to contemplate, let alone believe. But there it was plain and simple and an obvious choice, really. Could her government be behind it all? Could her own people have killed Osman and sent her running?

No, she would not believe it until she talked to her aunt. Aunt Hannah would know. She would help.

Her mind made up, Maya got out of bed and pocketed her meager belongings. Maybe she could find a pay phone nearby. If so, she could be under her aunt's protection within the hour.

With renewed energy, Maya hurried out of the flat and down the steps. The cool morning air washed over her as she scurried down the sidewalk, the faint smell of salt tickling her senses. She was so refreshed with elation and hope that her trade-craft failed her.

So, as she rushed past the corner and its line of plastic trashcans waiting for dutiful public servants, Maya never noticed the shadow in her midst until one gloved hand clamped over her mouth and another hand wrapped around her neck.

HAIFA, ISRAEL

August 28th, 5:03am IDT

Maya's body tensed and her barred teeth clamped down on the gloved hand. She heard the man curse and just as she went to break the hold, the man said, "Dammit, Maya, let go."

For some reason she listened to the order and bent to a crouch. As if on cue she heard a crack and shards of brick fell from where her head had just been.

"Run," the man urged, as if Maya needed the encouragement. He forcefully nudged her in the correct direction.

She didn't know the identity of the man who'd grabbed her but she wasn't exactly in a place to argue. Maya bolted, her legs churning as she heard more shots from behind. *Silenced weapon. Small caliber. Probably a twenty-two.*

Her mind reverted back to her training, endless hours spent familiarizing herself with a variety of weapons, and countless more hours spent firing them at various distances. While she'd never been shot at in real life, her instructors had fired plenty of rounds over their heads to get them used to the feel and the sounds as they attempted to find cover.

That's what she had to do now - find cover. You would

think it an easy thing to do in a city where cars and buildings were everywhere, but the angles were all wrong. Whoever was following her and the mystery man wasn't alone. She could feel them closing in like a pack of wolves. One attacker was probably right behind them while the other sounded like he was coming from the other side of the street. Angles. *Amateurs never thought enough about angles.*

Just then, she heard a squeal of tires and in her mind the current situation went from bad to worse. With no alleys to duck into and the street turns limited, she and her guardian angel could easily be overtaken.

"Get closer to the street," she heard the man say.

Maya was incredulous. "What? The car..."

"Just do it," the man ordered, overtaking her sprint with long sure strides. That was when she recognized him. There had been something in his voice but she hadn't been sure. It was in the way he ran; Maya had run behind him for too many miles to count. Although she was currently being chased and shot at, her outlook improved.

Maya heard the large engine and glanced right. Out of the corner of her eye she saw a dark vehicle, larger than a car, but she couldn't be sure. The man in front of her slowed and reached back with his hand. Maya took it and felt herself being pulled forward. Then as the van swerved in next to them the man flung her towards the open sliding door. She somehow made it through the door and into someone's waiting arms. The man came in next and he barked an order. The van door slammed shut as the driver gunned the engine and the van propelled forward.

Her rescuer was tossed unceremoniously to the back of the van, his body being tossed like a rag doll. Someone flicked on the overhead light and whoever was holding Maya asked, "Still in one piece?"

Rubbing his head from the collision with the back door, the man said, "I'm fine."

Maya went to him.

"Judah?!"

He grinned.

"When did you know it was me?" he asked.

"When you sprinted in front of me," Maya answered, returning his grin.

"Are you sure it wasn't when I whispered in your ear?"

Maya shook her head in exasperation but laughed. "You haven't changed one bit."

Judah shrugged, his youthful features taking Maya back to when she'd first met Judah Burns. They'd only been eighteen at the time, both fresh-faced and determined to graduate at the top of their basic training class. Rivals at the beginning, the two teenagers had soon found they had much in common, namely a proclivity for hard work and a natural talent for languages. On their down time the two would square off like live stand-up comedy. Maya was the master of American English, particularly from the deep south, and Judah did the most hilarious Russian impressions.

In the end, Judah graduated at the top of their class and Maya second. It was not the last time they would meet.

"It seems that I am now in your debt," she said.

"Does that mean you'll finally go on a date with me?" Judah did his best starry-eyed lover impression. It was always the same with Judah. While Maya considered herself pretty, and at times beautiful depending on the time of day, what she wore, and the amount of makeup she sometimes donned, Judah Burns could have been a model. He'd put those good looks to use not only with many of the women who couldn't resist his charms, but also he'd turned it into a tool in his current line of work.

"You're not still dating that French model, you know, the one with the rich daddy?"

Judah snorted like he had never done such a thing in his life.

"I would rather date someone who is beautiful and smarter than me," he said.

Maya bit back a blush, suddenly realizing that there were four other people listening in on their conversation. Reality came crashing down around her. The chase. The silenced rounds. Maya's mind snapped back to the business at hand – staying alive.

"How did you find me?"

The smile slipped from Judah's handsome face.

"I can't tell you."

He was serious. It was probably because his men were there.

"And who were the ones shooting at us?"

"I don't know."

Judah could be infuriating. One minute he was flirting with her and the next he was playing master of intrigue.

Maya glared at him but he did not budge.

"Can you at least tell me who sent you?"

Judah nodded, exchanging a glance with the man who'd caught her.

"Your aunt."

"Hannah?"

"Yes."

"How did *she* know where I was? I didn't..."

"It's not important, Maya."

She could have punched him in that moment. Of course it was important. She was a professional, and they'd tracked her down in a matter of hours. The thought sent shivers up and down her spine. Maya took a calming breath.

"Where are you taking me?"

"You'll see. I'll tell you everything when we get there."

Judah then got up and made his way to the front of the paneled van, plopping himself into the passenger seat. He could be so infuriating.

MAYA ESTIMATED THEY'D BEEN ON THE ROAD FOR JUST OVER twenty minutes when the van pulled curbside. One of Judah's men slid the side door open and held out his hand to help her out. She ignored it and stepped out onto a brightly lit sidewalk, immediately recognizing they had arrived at the airport.

Judah got out and motioned for her to follow. They'd walked fifty feet when he stopped and produced a large manila envelope from his coat.

"Your flight leaves in thirty minutes. It won't wait."

Maya unclasped the envelope and pulled out the smallest item - a passport. She opened it and found her own image staring back at her. It was her face accompanied with a new name. There was also a stack of stapled papers and a cashier's check made out to the person on the passport.

"I don't understand." she said. "Where am I going?"

"You're listed on the manifest as a courier with diplomatic privileges. The rest of the passengers are diplomats, lobbyists and low-level government employees. It's a private charter so it shouldn't be hard keeping to yourself."

"Judah, I don't understand. Where am I going?"

"To America."

"What? Why?"

"Your aunt thought it would be the safest place for you now."

America? Why America? And then his words sunk in.

"You said *for now*. When am I coming back?"

Judah looked away, pretending like he was scanning the area, but Maya knew better. He was avoiding her.

"I asked, when am I coming back?"

"I don't know, okay?" He looked as upset as she felt. "Look, I shouldn't be telling you this, but you're not safe here anymore. We have not identified the people who killed Colonel Osman or the ones who were following you. You have to board the plane now, Maya. Then read what's in the envelope."

"You haven't read it?"

"No. Your aunt said it was intended only for you."

"And is she safe?"

"Yes."

"Are you sure?" Maya pressed.

"She said she was as safe as possible."

There were so many questions that Maya wanted to ask. How she wished she could speak to Hannah. Maybe she could on the plane, or maybe once they'd landed.

"Maya, you need to go. They won't hold the plane."

She didn't want to be mad at Judah. It wasn't his fault this had happened. He'd even saved her life less than an hour before. But, he was the only person she could unleash her anger on.

"Fine, thanks."

She pushed past him, ignoring his goodbye. If she said anything she knew the tears would come.

Ten minutes later, she was sitting in the over-sized leather chair on the posh private charter, holding a mimosa in her hand. The plane taxied to the runway and Maya looked out the window as the first glimmers of light tickled the horizon. Judah was right where she'd left him, by the fence, watching her depart. He waved to the plane and without thinking she waved back even though he couldn't possibly see her. A moment later he retreated and returned to the black van.

The jet's engine growled as the pilot announced that they were about to take off. Maya's eyes were still glued on the van. Then, just as the jet roared to life and launched down the runway, Judah's van exploded in a fiery ball.

Maya let out a silent scream as the aircraft catapulted into the air.

WILD DUNES

Isle of Palms, South Carolina

AUGUST 28TH, 10:12AM

C al winced and put a hand to his eyes when he emerged from the master bedroom. The sunlight was blinding and it didn't help his pounding head.

"Good morning," a voice said from the nook just off the kitchen. It took Cal's addled mind a moment to realize it was Daniel. He squinted and saw the sniper reading a newspaper at the kitchen table.

"What time is it?" Cal asked, shuffling to the fridge.

"Just after ten."

"Is anyone else up?"

"Top stopped by after his run. Said he was picking up coffee and breakfast stuff for everybody."

Cal groaned at the thought of exercise and food. His body was not getting any younger and a night of hard drinking couldn't just be shaken off anymore. He'd given Diane the bed while he slept on the floor. That only added to his aches and pains.

Cal grabbed a glass from the cabinet and filled it with tap

water. He pounded one glass and then a second. It didn't help his rumbling stomach or the headache, but it did clear away some of the cobwebs.

He took a seat across from Daniel, easing his way down gingerly as he felt the prickles rack his skin.

"I hope you're happy," Cal mumbled.

"Happy about what?" Daniel asked.

Cal looked up in confusion. "What? Oh, no, sorry. I was thinking out loud. Actually, I was talking to Trav. Bastard wanted a throw-down party and I'd say we gave him one."

His memory of the end of the night was spotty. He did remember howling as Top did cartwheels down the beach and Gaucho followed with much less grace, more of a tumbling rock than a gymnast.

Daniel chuckled. "We've got one bottle left. You sure you don't want a little hair of the dog?"

Cal gave him a disgusted look followed by a middle finger.

The sound of the master bedroom opening made Cal swivel in his chair. He felt his heart race a few beats faster. While he didn't remember everything that had happened during the party, he could clearly see Diane's face in the fire-light. She'd enjoyed herself as much as the rest of the team, but they'd said maybe ten words to one another last night, and five of those were, "You can have the bed."

Diane came out of the master bedroom with sunglasses in her hand. She quickly put them on when the sun assaulted her senses.

"Please tell me you have coffee," she said, trudging into the kitchen.

"Top's gone to get some," Cal said.

Diane nodded and flopped down in the seat next to Cal. Without asking, she grabbed his half-full glass and chugged the water.

"I can't remember the last time I had that much to drink,"

Diane said, handing the glass to Cal and motioning for more water. Cal was happy to comply.

"Daniel says we didn't kill it all. Can I interest you in a shot of Jack to go with your water?"

Diane rolled her eyes with a moan. She chugged the second glass like a recruit at boot camp and then stood up suddenly.

"I need to go for a walk," she said, looking to Cal. "Coming?"

Cal nodded and tried to ignore the sly grin on Daniel's face.

"Let me get my sunglasses."

THE COOL BREEZE COMING OFF THE ATLANTIC GREETED the pair as they emerged from the sandy path and stepped out onto the beach. It was probably 75 degrees but with the wind it felt more like 65 degrees.

They walked north, neither saying a word as they skirted the surf through ankle-deep water. Cal thought about all the times he'd walked the same stretch of beach during the preceding months. Not once had he felt the way he did now, his feet tingling from bubbling surf and his nose inhaling the perfect salt air. He felt like he was coming back to life. Everything felt new and untainted.

And then there was Diane. He suddenly felt the overwhelming urge to hold her, to smell her hair and taste her lips. But he didn't do any of those things. Instead he kept walking.

"How have you been?" he asked after he'd finally gotten up the nerve to speak.

"How do you think I've been?" she said, an edge to her tone that she'd never leveled at him. "I'm sorry." Diane stopped. Her right hand reached out and touched his arm. "I shouldn't have said that."

Cal shook his head.

"It's my fault. I'm the one who ran away."

"You were in pain."

"I was, but it wasn't fair just leaving you like that. I can't imagine how that made you feel."

Diane let out a nervous laugh. "It wasn't pretty. I was a wreck. Top would stop by every couple of days to check on me. He was really sweet and he even brought me dinner when he could tell I wasn't eating." The thought of Diane in pain made Cal's heart ache. *He'd done this to her.* "But I got through it. We all did. Jonas said I could stop by The Jefferson Group whenever I wanted and for a while I did. I hope they didn't get sick of me. I just...I had this crazy feeling that one day you'd walk through the front door and everything would be exactly like it had been." Diane's voice trailed off sending the dagger deeper into Cal's gut. He took her hand in his. She didn't let go.

"The day Trav died, a part of me died too," Cal said, vocalizing the pain that he was only now beginning to comprehend. "He was the only family I had left. He was more like my brother and for months the only way I could remember him was from the last time I saw him with blood on his face and those eyes staring into nothingness —" The image stormed into his brain but this time he was able to push it away replacing it with a happier memory of the good times he'd had with his cousin. "I've lost people before, only this time it felt so final, like everything had been taken. I wasn't in a place mentally where I could be any good to you. I honestly never expected you to talk to me again."

Diane squeezed his hand. "I'm here now."

"I know."

"And you were wrong."

"About what?"

"You have family. Neil, Top, Jonas and the rest of your guys. I mean, the president is one of your best friends. You're not alone, Cal. You'll never be alone."

"What about you? Are we still friends?" The words felt childish, but Cal didn't care. Diane nodded. "Is there a chance we can be more than friends again?"

Diane stepped closer and said, "We'll take it slow, okay?"

Hope sprouted in Cal's chest, warm and inviting. Her answer was more than he'd believed himself worthy of.

"I'm good with slow," he said.

Diane grinned. "But not too slow." She squeezed his hand again and they stood there for a minute, just enjoying the morning and each other.

By the time they arrived back at the house, Diane had filled Cal in on her studies and her career path. She'd graduated from UVA in May and was temporarily assigned to the Naval ROTC unit until a slot opened up for the Naval Intelligence basic course in Dam Neck, Virginia. Cal was happy that she was pursuing her dream to be an intelligence officer. Her experience as an enlisted intelligence analyst would only add to her considerable skill as an officer. She'd be a valuable asset to any command, and at one point Cal had even entertained offering her a position within TJG. Maybe it was better that they kept their professional lives separate.

They were still holding hands when they entered Cal's vacation rental. The Secret Service agent at the door nodded a curt hello and said something into his mic. Cal and Diane followed the sounds of happy chatter and the smells of coffee and breakfast.

When they entered the kitchen, the whole gang was there. They were spread around the room eating bagels and sipping coffee, everyone except Daniel. Trent and the Secret Service agents looked like they'd just woken up. The president was sitting on the couch nursing a mug of coffee as he talked with Jonas. They both looked up when Cal and Diane walked in.

"Well, good morning, sunshine," Cal said, letting go of Diane's hand and taking a seat next to Brandon. Diane went in search for coffee.

"I think Travis would've been proud of the mess we made of ourselves," Brandon said, rubbing his head like it would help the pounding.

"How's your detail feel about it?"

Brandon chuckled.

"I don't think they're too happy about the leader of the free world getting hammered, but they'll get over it."

Diane was back a second later with a mug of steaming coffee for Cal. He took it gratefully and Diane left to give them some privacy.

"So, what's new? What did I miss during my sabbatical?" Cal asked, taking a sip of his coffee.

"Have you not seen the news?" Brandon asked, one eyebrow raised.

"No, not a bit."

Brandon and Jonas exchanged amused looks.

"Let's just say that in your absence I've somehow managed to stir up a virtual hornet's nest on the world stage."

"Would you care to elaborate?"

Brandon nodded and told him about the speech at the U.N. and the resulting tsunami of confusion.

"What brought that up? Something you've been planning for a while?" Cal asked, surprised that his friend would go out on such a shaky limb. It wasn't that he didn't agree with Brandon, but to say those things in a public forum, and especially at the United Nations of all places seemed more than a bit out of bounds.

"Would you believe me if I said I thought it's what you and Travis would've done?"

"You're serious?"

"I am."

"But you're the president. Aren't you supposed to be more politically correct than us dumb grunts?"

"Watch who you're calling a dumb grunt!" Trent bellowed from across the room. It seemed that everyone was listening in.

"I guess I just thought that I needed to shake things up."

"Well you sure did that!" laughed Gaucho from his perch at the bar.

"So what's your plan?" Cal asked, warming to the idea as his mind continued to wake after months of long hibernation.

"Well, I was just talking to Jonas about that. Now that you're back, I was hoping you guys could help us track down some of our leads."

"What leads?"

"We're already seeing a lot of money being moved, lots of chatter in social media and over the cell networks. The NSA and CIA are working overtime to find the commonalities to gather the intel we can exploit."

"So, what you're saying is that you beat the bushes and now the rats are running for new places to hide," Cal said, imagining the panic in places like Iraq, where U.S. dollars had filled the pockets of officials and criminals alike.

Brandon nodded.

"I've told agency directors to prioritize the actionable intelligence with the biggest targets first. When we take down the first handful of bad guys, I want to make sure it hits the media with a bang."

Cal imagined the possibilities. They could be busy for

decades. Finally, someone was doing something to lift the veil and expose the darkness. Cal felt the familiar urge to grab a gun and jump on a plane. He was about to ask Brandon where he thought the first targets might be when the Secret Service agent positioned at the front door rushed into the room. Everyone turned.

"Mr. President, there's a young lady downstairs who would like a word with you."

The special agent looked uncomfortable like he'd just told the president that there was a naked woman downstairs. Half the room got up from their chairs.

"Who is it and how did she find me?" the president asked patiently.

"I don't know, sir. She said she could only tell you." The large man's unease grew with every word. Cal could tell it was taking enormous effort for the man to get the syllables out of his mouth. Now the whole room was standing.

The president's calm demeanor slipped for just a moment.

"There better be a damned good reason for this."

This time the special agent actually gulped.

"Sir, she's here with the Israeli Ambassador."

WILD DUNES

Isle of Palms, South Carolina

AUGUST 28TH, 11:49AM

The young woman walked into the room preceded by the Israeli Ambassador, flanked by two Secret Service agents. Her eyes darted around the room. She looked like a caged animal, afraid and disheveled. Zimmer noticed the manila envelope she had clutched tightly to her chest like a mother protecting her baby.

Zimmer's musings were cut short by the Israeli Ambassador, who the president considered a friend.

"Mr. President, I am so sorry for disturbing you." His accent was pure American English. He'd lived in the U.S. since he was a child due to his father's diplomatic posts in and around Washington, D.C. In many ways, Sandy Ullman was as American as the rest of the men and women in the room. He was also a career diplomat and if he was concerned by the amount of muscle in the room he didn't show it. "Is there a place we can talk privately?"

Maybe it was the hangover or maybe the fact that he

wasn't in the mood for pleasantries but Zimmer was in no condition to play games.

"Anything you need to say to me you can say in front of my friends." He felt a stinging headache coming on. "How did you know I was here, Sandy?"

"The CIA," Ullman replied, as if it were no big deal.

It was no secret that Israel had a long history of spying on the United States. From commercial innovation to military intelligence, their forces were well-entrenched in American society. But to hear that the CIA had given Ullman his private location...

"I am simply here to make the introduction. Mr. President, may I present Maya Eilenberg?"

There were no handshakes, only nods from Eilenberg and the president. Zimmer could feel the rest of the room looking on with unabashed curiosity.

"Why don't we have a seat at the table, Ms. Eilenberg," Zimmer said. A way parted between the rest of the observers. "Can I get you anything?"

"Thank you, no," she answered in a hoarse voice.

Zimmer poured her a glass of water anyway, and Top produced a plate of Danishes.

"Mr. President," the Ambassador said, "I'll leave you to chat with Ms. Eilenberg. My return flight to D.C. is waiting."

"But aren't you going to...?" Zimmer started to ask.

Ullman put his hands in the air. "I was instructed to make the introduction and, in case you were wondering, I do not know what Ms. Eilenberg is going to discuss with you. My *friend* thought it would be best."

Zimmer didn't argue. He was safe with Cal and the rest of The Jefferson Group in attendance. Besides, he was more than a little curious as to A) why the Israelis would go to such lengths to find him, and B) what this young woman had clutched so tightly in her hands.

"We'll make sure she gets back to D.C.," Zimmer said.

Ullman nodded and left without another word. All eyes were fixed on Maya Eilenberg. Zimmer found it interesting that even though she looked like she'd been through something traumatic, she did not cower. There was fear in her eyes, but it wasn't directed at him or the other people in the room.

"May I call you Maya?" Zimmer asked.

"Yes, Mr. President." She had but only a slight accent.

Zimmer smiled. "Why don't you tell me why you're here, Maya."

With the envelope still held against her chest, Maya said, "I had the whole flight over to think about what I should say, and now that I am here I do not know what to say."

"Why don't you start at the beginning?"

Maya exhaled and the envelope was lowered slowly to the table.

"For the past two years I worked for a man named Osman. He was a Colonel in the Israeli army and spent many years with intelligence. He never told me so, but I believe he did time with Mossad and Shin Bet. Colonel Osman handpicked a team of security and intelligence specialists to be part of a secret project. Osman told us that the operation was tasked from the highest levels of the Israeli government, and that its success would ensure the future of our country. Naturally, as patriotic men and women, we jumped at the opportunity. I had been an intelligence analyst stuck behind a computer day and night. This was my chance to give back or so I thought."

Maya grabbed the glass of water and took a sip. She gazed into the water like she was watching her memories unfold.

"We received training before the project got underway and our team went from twenty to fifteen members. Osman was impressed with my abilities and made me his deputy. It wasn't until then that I got a glimpse of what our job entailed. Mostly, it consisted of surveying the activities of a single man, a geologist and inventor named Dr. Aviel Nahas. We monitored his movements, tracked his computer usage, and even followed him on his free time. Colonel Osman liked to make surprise visits to the doctor's lab. He said it would keep Nahas on his toes, which it did. For almost a year, that was all we did. No one except Osman knew what Nahas was building. I saw the occasional sketch or schematic, but whatever he was doing was well hidden. I came to find out that was Osman's doing, as a precautionary measure, should pieces of the research fall into the wrong hands."

"One day, Osman called me into his office. He seemed distracted, maybe even worried. He said he shouldn't be telling me, but that he had to, that he couldn't be the only one on our team to know the information. Osman showed me Nahas's plans and even let me look at the pictures from the manufacturing facility where they were taking the plans and building prototypes in real time. The final replica looked like a horseshoe crab. Do you know what they are?"

Zimmer nodded. "Hard-dome shell? Spiked tail? Lots of feet? They have them here in South Carolina."

"Yes. Well, I had never seen them. Osman showed me pictures of the real thing. But the ones Nahas was building were much larger."

"How big?" Zimmer asked.

"Approximately thirty-feet long and just under that in width."

"I don't understand. What was it they were planning on using them for?"

Maya looked uncomfortable for a moment but regained her composure and asked, "How much do you know about deep sea mining?"

"I've been briefed on it a few times. I know that it's been

highly cost prohibitive, mostly due to the sheer depth you have to go to in order to hit the right pockets." Zimmer didn't mention the environmental implications.

"That is true. Up until ten years ago, very few companies had ever taken more than a few samples from the deepest reaches of the world's oceans. But now, with the increased use of rare earth elements, of which China holds over ninety percent of the known land-based mines, companies and nations are looking to find these untapped resources and bring them to market."

Zimmer knew all about rare earth elements (REEs). Not a week went by that some lobbyist wasn't begging him to expand America's reach in order to combat the stranglehold China had on the rare earth market. Everything from computer chips to glass tint required REEs for manufacturing.

"So, what are you saying? What do these things do, exactly?"

"Nahas originally designed them as exploration vehicles. As his trials progressed, his optimism grew, as did the size of the prototypes. Ultimately, he believed that swarms of these vehicles could be used to mine and deliver the raw elements from the bottom of the ocean."

Zimmer knew that one of the problems with deep sea mining was delivery. In the past, there were two options. You could either use a continuous line bucket system or a hydraulic suction system. Again, the extreme depths of proposed mining sites always kept either system from becoming reality.

"Okay. So this Nahas came up with a way to get to the prize. What does this have to do with us?"

A shadow seemed to pass across Maya's face. She looked down at her hands.

"Osman explained that tapping into these deep sea mines

could mean a flood of money for Israel. We have long been known for our expertise within supply chains like diamond and gold but we have never really owned the source. This would be our chance to own the supply." Maya shook her head, eyes still downcast. "Part of the plan was to exploit your exclusive economic zones through American intermediaries. The same would happen across the globe in locations where potential mines would be located."

Zimmer did not understand. While the plan might sound like an economic coup of sort, surely it wasn't important enough to have this young woman fly halfway around the world to brief him.

"Maya, I'm still not sure what this means."

She looked up. This time there were tears in her eyes.

"Colonel Osman was murdered. I have been on the run for days. And yesterday, as my plane was taking off from Haifa, I watched a friend and his team get killed when their vehicle exploded."

She'd lain them out like playing cards, as if she were still trying to make sense of the hand she'd been dealt.

The entire room had seen all manner of evil committed for money but to Zimmer there was still something missing. As if reading his mind, Maya finally said, "I've been sent to ask for your help."

"Help with what?"

"All the prototypes and the plans have been stolen, Mr. President."

Again, that didn't sound like it was America's problem.

"What does this have to do with us, Ms. Eilenberg?"

This time her gaze did not waver.

"I was told to give you one name."

"And what name is that?"

Zimmer wasn't sure if he saw the hint of a grin or the beginning of a grimace on the Israeli's face.

"Hannah Krygier," she said, slowly, like sap dripping from a maple tree.

His body froze and the blood drained from the president's face. That was a name he'd hoped never to hear again.

WILD DUNES

Isle of Palms, South Carolina

Maya stared at President Zimmer's startled expression. He looked shell-shocked, and the Israeli couldn't understand why. Her aunt's instructions had been clear. "*Tell him my name and everything will fall into place*," the handwritten note had said. Maya had expected it to be like an introduction from afar.

"Can you say that name again, please?" the president said, pronouncing each word like he was asking for a secret password.

"Hannah Krygier," Maya repeated slowly.

Zimmer nodded his head, his face grave, but his composure had returned. He motioned to one of the men who had escorted her and the ambassador in.

"Please find Ms. Eilenberg a room. I need to make a phone call." Then he turned back to Maya. "Thank you for your visit. Now if you'll excuse me, I have to see to my duties."

He grabbed the envelope from the table and flashed her a

smile. Maya could see it was forced. Whatever her aunt's name had dredged up, it now had the president's undivided attention.

Maya stood from the table and left with the Secret Service agent. The adrenaline was wearing thin and her feet felt heavy and clumsy. A shower and a nap were all she could think about as she tried to ignore the curious gazes of the crowded room of onlookers.

* * *

"WHAT THE HELL WAS THAT ABOUT?" TRENT WHISPERED TO Cal once the center of attention had left.

"I don't know, but did you see his face?"

Trent nodded. They'd been through some close calls with the president but neither man had seen their friend's countenance change in the blink of an eye.

"Let me go talk to him," Cal said.

He made his way to the master bedroom where the president had decided to make his phone call. Upon entering the room Cal saw the manila envelope, now open, with its contents laying on the bed. Brandon was pacing back and forth, his secure phone in his right hand and a single sheet of paper in his left.

"I want to know everything you've got on Israeli agents currently working within our borders." There was a pause as he listened to whomever was on the other end. "No, it's fine that you told him where I was. It's *that* important." Another brief pause and then the president said, "Call me as soon as you know."

Brandon ended the call and threw the phone on the bed. For a moment he didn't even acknowledge Cal's presence.

"Who was that?" Cal asked.

"The CIA."

"Do you want to tell me what's going on?"

Brandon didn't answer.

Cal looked down at the papers the Eilenberg girl had delivered. There were dossiers and maps; some information was redacted in heavy black. If there was a common thread to the documents, it wasn't immediately evident. It looked more like a random compilation of information - like pieces from several jigsaw puzzles thrown into one box.

"Did I ever tell you what they gave me when I inherited the presidency?" Brandon inquired.

"I don't think so."

"So, they bring you into this little room where you have to sign your initials in a thousand places, have your picture taken, get scanned for retina recognition, and I think they even took a few vials of blood. Well, when that's all done they bring in the presidential briefers. I'm actually surprised that no one has quit after all the information they impart. If the American people knew what I know..." Brandon shivered at the thought. "So, after the doom and gloom of the bad news, they try to provide some good news. One of the things these experts will tell a new president is where our assets are located. They're very thorough going into great detail about what countries we've infiltrated most successfully and where we have the most influence both economically and militarily. Then one of them handed me a single card with five names. The card had names and the country associated with the name. I was told to memorize the names and once I did the guy burned the card immediately."

"And that lady's name was on the card?"

"Yeah."

Cal waited for the punch line but Brandon had once again drifted back to his thoughts.

"So you don't know her?" Cal asked. The president shook his head. "Then who is she?"

"She's a mole."

"Here in the U.S.?"

"No, in Israel."

"But why? How long has she been working for us?"

"She doesn't exactly work *for* us. The way it was explained to me, this person acts like an early warning system, coming above ground only to alert us of a dire emergency. They told me that these sources are considered as one-time uses. Once their cover is blown, that's it," Brandon explained. "No one knows about them except the president and the source. Up until now I assumed they'd disappeared or died."

"But we've got spies all over the world. Hell, we tap anything we can get our hands on. Are you telling me that these people are better than that?"

"Honestly, I don't know. The presidential handlers didn't exactly give me a detailed game plan. It was more of a "what if" deal. I do remember them saying that our relationships with these sources were developed in the late sixties. I have no idea how they were selected, or how it could be known they would rise to high-ranking positions of power. But what I do know is that each person on the note card had the ability to attain certain vital information whose authenticity would not be questioned."

There were too many questions to ask. Cal picked the first that popped into his head.

"So, why now? Is it because of this deep-sea thing? Do you really think it's that big a deal?"

"No. I don't think it has anything to do with mining rare resources."

"Then what?"

The president's voice sounded cold and his face hardened like a general preparing for battle.

"These sources were put in place to prevent calamity. Specifically, they're there to warn us should the established order within their country collapse to the point of breaking. But, it would have to be something hidden, something our usual sources couldn't sniff out."

Cal was starting to understand. No country was perfect and nut jobs cropped up all too often. They rose in popularity, fueled by dissension, riding the waves of national rejuvenation when in fact these power mongers just wanted control. Cal couldn't think of anyone like that in Israel but maybe he was out of touch.

"What do you want us to do?" Cal asked, correctly assuming the president would want The Jefferson Group in on the action.

"I want you to take this stuff," Brandon said, pointing to the documents, "and find out what the hell is going on. I want you to find out why Israel wants to start a war with the United States of America."

HAIFA, ISRAEL

Four Hours Earlier

"It will work."

Hannah Krygier stared calmly at the man sitting across from her. He sipped his glass of champagne like a debutante. She hated him and would have loved to snatch the glass from his hand, smash it across his face, and stab the exposed stem into his temple. The thought made her smile. The smile turned into a chuckle.

"You don't believe me?" the man said, obviously misinterpreting her mirth. Hannah was glad for it.

"I did not say that. I merely stated the facts."

"Hannah, please do not tell me that you are having doubts."

The comment made her smile disappear. She glowered at the man.

"I told you not to move up the timetable; you ignored me. I told you I could handle Ozzy; you ignored me again. Tell me Efraim, why is it that I am still here? Maybe you should place one of those discreet calls and have *me* killed."

This time her visitor chuckled.

"Oh, Hannah. Let us discuss something more cheerful, like the way Zimmer is playing into our hands."

Hannah clenched her fists under the table and willed the shaking to stop. How she hated this man. The thought of Maya, who would soon be talking to President Zimmer, made her body relax.

"The American may be acting like a fool but do not forget what he has accomplished in his short time as president," Hannah said, sipping her chardonnay. "Maybe you are right; it may be the perfect time. I apologize for doubting your judgment."

Her apology was accepted with a slow nod.

"Our people say he has his intelligence assets refocused on his new legacy plan. This shift will help us achieve our goal without the scrutiny we might otherwise have encountered."

"And the vessels?"

Efraim's grin widened.

"They near their targets even as we speak."

* * *

HANNAH STOOD AT HER FRONT DOOR AND WATCHED THE armored SUV roll through the iron gate. She stepped inside, closed the door, and locked it. She then slid to the floor, her energy spent. The sobs were gone. The tears were spent, but the pain was still there. The pain and the anger were what kept her moving.

She thought of the assassin's face, the one who had stepped so casually through the same door she was sitting against now. He had informed her that her ex-husband was dead and that a team would arrive in minutes to dispose of the body to clean up the courtyard. No one had forewarned her of the decision. So, as her face remained placid, her heart had broken.

Ozzy was her first love. He was a gruff man, a soldier accustomed to getting his way which had ultimately ended their marriage. But they'd remained friends, and over the years she noticed the lingering gaze or the kiss on the cheek that lasted a second too long.

She'd brought him in on the operation because he was the right man for the job. If anyone could keep Nahas's research and development under wraps, it was Ozzy.

But they'd lied to her. They'd told her that once the initial phase was complete, Col. Osman and his team would simply be reassigned. Most of the team had received new assignments, except Osman and Maya. According to Efraim, they knew too much.

She'd failed to warn Osman, but at least she had succeeded in warning Maya. It had been almost impossible to get her to America and it almost hadn't happened. Even now they were looking for her. Hannah could only hope that her good friend, Ambassador Ullman, would come through on his promise and deliver Maya to President Zimmer. He was her only hope. She had no idea how high up the conspiracy went. Hannah doubted the prime minister, her brother, was involved but Efraim and his cohorts would surely know if she contacted him.

It felt like they knew everything. They'd somehow tracked down Maya and casually killed Judah Burns and his men outside the airport. The unofficial statement from government sources said the explosion was the result of a Palestinian bomb. They'd even released photos of the suspected suicide bombers to the media.

Hannah knew that the story would vanish in short order. It was the way of things. The world and her people had become desensitized to the violence. The news that topped the "trending" list today would soon be covered by the garbage of Internet slush within a matter of mere hours.

Hannah thought about handsome Judah, Maya's friend, who'd done her a personal favor. His men hadn't known who they were working for but they followed him into danger. They'd lost their lives due to their blind faith. Hannah could only hope that Maya would begin to unravel the twisted tale that was just now beginning to wind its way around the world. The only people who could help her now were the Americans.

* * *

THE ARMORED SUV PULLED UP TO THE GOVERNMENT utility van sitting a block from the house that it had just left. The passenger side window rolled down and a bearded face appeared.

"Has she made any calls?" Efraim Perlstein asked from the back seat of the SUV.

"Only for work."

"Any visitors?"

"Just you."

Perlstein nodded. "Call me if you notice anything out of the ordinary and I mean *anything*. Do you understand?"

"I understand."

Perlstein rolled up his window and motioned for the driver to leave. As the SUV rolled toward its next destination, the former Information Minister of Israel's mind drifted back to the conversation he'd just had with the fascinating Hannah Krygier. Not only was she beautiful, but also she'd managed to bridge the divide between warring political parties during her time in government service. She'd come highly recommended and she passed every test they'd given her. That was no small feat considering the fact that Hannah Krygier was the highest-placed female in their little plot. She had earned her rank, and one of the reasons for Perlstein's visit was to see if she still deserved the position.

After all, who wouldn't place a bit of careful scrutiny on a colleague who'd just lost her ex-husband and a woman she considered a niece went missing. It was better to investigate such a colleague and assign judgment later.

Perlstein was not a patient man but he knew the significance of having Krygier on their side. It was not every day that you had the Israeli Prime Minister's sister in a noose.

WILD DUNES

Isle of Palms, South Carolina

AUGUST 28TH, 3:15PM

"I think we should fly to Tel Aviv," Trent said, receiving nods from many in the room. The president had left soon after Maya's revelation, and he would coordinate the efforts in D.C. That left The Jefferson Group and SSI teams gathered in Cal's vacation home, brainstorming. The coffee machine was on constant drip, and take-out food littered the living and dining rooms. The mood was grim but focused.

Cal let the others take the lead. His brain was still awakening from its self-imposed stasis. For the last two hours he'd listened and processed the discussion while he searched through the contents of Maya's mysterious envelope.

There were names, locations and grainy photographs that could have been Cold War-era memorabilia. It simply looked like a compilation of random notes. Cal wondered if they were the work of Hannah Krygier and he had asked Maya as much. She said she didn't know but that it was certainly possible.

For her part, Maya answered questions when she could. It didn't look like she was holding anything back but it was against every fiber in Cal's body to trust a stranger completely, regardless of the situation.

Neil had three laptops running simultaneously and he was doing what he did best, processing buckets of information like a squirrel sorting nuts. He'd loaded the pertinent information from Maya's files, but so far nothing. Every couple of minutes he'd come up for air, take a sip of coffee, and then return to work. He was like a bloodhound that had yet to find the scent.

"Hey, Maya, can you tell us again about how they planned to launch these 'bug' things?" Gaucho asked. Ever since seeing the picture of a horseshoe on Neil's computer screen, the Hispanic operator insisted that it looked like a bug.

"Dr. Nahas's notes suggested using either an exploration vessel or a salvage ship. As far as I know the delivery vehicle was never finalized," Maya answered.

"And these pictures?" Daniel held up a photocopied page from the files. "You've never seen these ships before?"

"No. I've never seen those images or ships."

Cal stared at the picture in his hand. It was grainy and obscured, but it was most definitely a ship. It was hard to make out the exact shape. The photograph had been taken at night, and the angles were obscured like it had been taken from a reflection in a shattered mirror. Neil was running it through his recognition program.

"And what about all these names and places?" Trent asked. "Do any of them ring a bell?"

Maya shook her head. They'd been over the same questions before. Cal saw the strain etched on her face.

"I wish I knew," she said. "It would be so much easier if I could call my aunt."

She'd mentioned her relationship to Krygier before but she had stopped short of elaborating; Cal needed to know.

"You keep referring to her as your aunt," he said. It was the first words he'd spoken since deliberations began.

"She's not really my aunt. I don't know how they met, but she knew my parents before I was born. They were more casual acquaintances than anything. I never met her until it was time to decide what I wanted to do after my time in the service. My father wanted me to get out of the service and return to school. My mother wanted me to find a nice boy and get married. I wanted to work in intelligence or possibly in the government." Maya chuckled. "Thinking he was helping his own cause, my father put me in touch with Hannah. She later told me that my father begged her to tell me all the bad things that could happen in either field. When I met her, she started to do as she'd promised, but by the time lunch was over she was giving me advice on which areas to explore and which she could possibly help me get into. I think she saw herself in me. After that day, she took an active role in my life. She never pressed and she never helped without me asking, similar to a benevolent aunt. That's why I started calling her Aunt Hannah, sort of as a joke, but it stuck."

"And she's the prime minister's sister?" Cal asked. Neil had provided that little tidbit seconds after Maya's earlier revelation.

"She is."

Someone had suggested calling the prime minister but that idea was shot down quickly. Until they had actionable intel, no one would be alerted. Those were the president's orders.

"Do you think the prime minister could be part of this?" Cal asked.

"Last week I would have said no, but now, I really do not know," Maya answered with a frown. "My life as I knew it seems to have been a highly crafted lie."

Cal thumbed through the files again. What were they missing? There had to be something, maybe some hidden message from Krygier buried under the mundane. Or maybe it was just a pile of red herrings.

"There is one thing that concerns me," Maya said, her voice detached as if she'd just remembered. "I never got the feeling that the Israelis were the ones doing all the work. Yes, we had Dr. Nahas, but where were they building the proto-types? Who was providing the vessels for final delivery? I asked Colonel Osman once, and he told me he did not know."

"Did you believe him?"

"I did. Once he brought me into his confidence, he told me everything. He even expressed his frustration that our employers were not providing him with sufficient informa-tion. One day I heard him growling into the phone, demanding to be given more access in order to provide adequate support. I did not hear the reply but judging from his demeanor the remainder of the day I could tell they had put him in his place."

It sounded like any number of government entities or higher headquarters that Cal had dealt with in the past. To the ones in charge it was called compartmentalization. To the troops on the ground it just felt like high school all over again, where only the popular kids got the good stuff. There was nothing worse than going into combat without a clear picture of what you were fighting for. The standard answer was to wave the flag in your face and say it was for King and Country. Cal assumed that Osman's handlers had given him the same message.

There were too many questions to ask. It was like being

given the key to a secure locker without the knowledge of where to find the locker or what lay within it.

Before Cal could press Maya for more information, Neil snapped his fingers and motioned to his computer. Cal moved to where he could see the image of what they'd assumed was a ship. There was another picture on the second screen, but this one was crisp and clear. It clearly showed a port, and the photograph had probably been taken from a plane. There were boats moored all throughout the crowded harbor, but two shapes immediately jumped out at Cal. The first was obviously an American aircraft carrier. Cal wasn't sure which one it was, but he could tell by the shape that it was American.

That wasn't the amazing part of the picture. Moored across the waterway from the Navy behemoth was something not as large but equally as impressive.

"Is that what I think it is?" Cal asked.

"If you think it's a yacht, yes, that's what you think it is." It wasn't just a yacht. It was a super-yacht. "Her name is *Nightshade* and she measures 180 meters. That's just under 600 feet for you non-metric boys, and she is currently the largest super-yacht in the world. She was built in Germany last year and is currently based in the Bahamas."

"That's what this is?" Cal asked, pointing to the original photo.

"I'm ninety-two percent sure of it," Neil said.

Daniel slid in next to Cal.

"Who owns that thing?" Daniel asked. Cal felt a chill run up his back.

Neil squinted at the screen. "A British national named Chance Baxter."

"The billionaire?" Dr. Higgins asked. No one else seemed to know the name, but Neil confirmed that *Sir* Chance was indeed on the list of world's billionaires.

Finally, a piece of the puzzle. Cal's brain clicked on and he felt the familiar vibration of synapses buzzing in his head along with a tingle of anticipation in his chest. He leaned forward and asked, "Neil, can you tell us where Sir Chance is *right* now?"

GREAT SALE CAY

The Bahamas

AUGUST 28TH, 5:44PM

Chancellor Brighton Baxter IV (known to the world as Chance Baxter) sometimes wore ear plugs to dull the sounds of the screaming. The soundproof room could contort the shrieks of a dying man. Not that they'd all been men, but the stray woman had been a rarity. His father had had a strange attraction to the Bahamian locals that peddled their wares in nearby Freeport, but to the current head of the Baxter empire such sexual proclivity had no place in the custom-made room on the northern end of his private island.

No, this was all business. It always was. If there was anything that anyone could say about Chance Baxter, it was that he was all business.

He stared at the mutilated corpse for a long moment, admiring his handiwork, and grinning back at the teeth that no longer had lips to cover them. The man had been tough and he had almost made it through the surgical precision of Baxter's deli-thin slices off the man's abdomen. He'd passed out after that, and it had taken two ampules of smelling salts to bring the man back to his senses.

After that Chance was like a butcher preparing a carcass. The man moaned and let out the occasional scream while Baxter hummed and carved away.

He liked to feed his local staff, and he still couldn't believe they hadn't realized that the delicate morsels he fed them for Sunday suppers were their fellow man. Ah, the irony of it all. Prehistoric meals for Bahamian savages. He grinned wider at the thought. Maybe a nice chimichurri sauce to go along with the man's flesh?

Baxter grabbed the hose that sat coiled in the corner, turned on the spigot, and rinsed his hands. The blood was starting to congeal, and it would make the unstrapping process a bother. Once satisfied, he walked back to the grinning corpse and undid the ankle straps, followed by the straps around the shins, then the waist strap, and on up until the last tie-down was the dead man's head. It was the only thing that kept the body from falling over. He'd learned that trick years ago. Better to let the cadaver's own weight do the job rather than having to heave the body in.

He moved to the nearest wall and depressed the black button that opened the hatch in the floor six inches in front of the bolted chair. The hatch door eased open revealing a hidden lagoon below. Baxter flipped a switch and LED lights lit up the water twenty feet below him. The blue space appeared empty at first and, then as if called by a silent dinner bell, the sharks came.

Baxter grabbed a piece of the dead man's cheek from the workbench and tossed it into the void. When it hit the water there was a flurry of activity, each predator snapping at the tiny snack in a frenzy.

"Have patience, my friends. More will be along shortly."

By the time he'd packaged a good portion of the rest of

the meat and put it in an ice-filled cooler, close to one hundred sharks had gathered in the underground cave. Baxter licked his lips in anticipation and unsnapped the only thing holding the corpse from its final resting place. Aided by the still-slick blood, it slipped down the chair, the feet going in first and the head last after a hollow smack against the corner of the portal.

Baxter watched as three sharks, one a giant hammerhead, sprang from the choppy water and pulled the body in. The billionaire looked at his watch and noted the time. It took the gathering only one minute and forty-four seconds to tear the body apart. Then he went about hosing off the room from top-to-bottom. Once every trace of blood and gore was safely in the lagoon below he stripped down naked, tossed his soiled clothes into the hole, and then hosed himself off. After giving the sharks a quick salute, Baxter closed the trap door and turned off the LED lights.

In the corner there was a towel and a clean robe in plastic wrap. He took his time dabbing his well-tanned body dry before wrapping himself in the spotless robe.

He let himself out after extinguishing the overhead lights. After the heavy door hissed closed, he pressed a button outside the hidden chamber which triggered the sanitizing showers that would complete the decontamination process. The next time he used the room it would be sterilized and fresh.

Baxter exhaled like a man who'd just climbed out after a long soothing soak in a hot tub. With the wet towel over one shoulder and the meat-packed cooler under one arm, he made his way down the dimly lit corridor that only he, master of the island, could access. When he emerged into the sunlight of the waning afternoon, there was a glass of champagne waiting. He ignored it and instead rang the tiny silver bell that sat on the same tray.

A moment later, a diminutive black man wearing a starched white suit appeared.

"Yes, Mr. Baxter?"

"George, would you please escort Dr. Nahas to my office?"

"The one on the first or third level, Mr. Baxter?"

Chance Baxter tapped his chin and then said, "Make it the third floor. I have a sudden urge to watch the sunset. Please bring up a bottle of gin."

"Yes, Mr. Baxter."

"Oh, and, George, would you take this cooler and deposit its contents into the deep freezer?"

"Right away, Mr. Baxter. Was it a good catch?"

The servant only knew it was meat, either something his master imported from England or something he'd caught on his frequent sailing expeditions.

"Yes, George, it was a very good catch. Thank you for asking."

George smiled and took the cooler. Baxter smiled back and grabbed the glass of champagne as his house manager left the room.

Yes, after all that work it would be good to watch the sunset. He did not care much whether Dr. Nahas would enjoy it. They did have business to discuss. More importantly, how would they deal with the act of sabotage he'd just uncovered?

THE WHITE HOUSE

August 28th, 6:38pm

Bob Lundgren barked another order into the phone. "And make sure you get it right this time."

Despite his outward appearance, the White House Press Secretary was finally beginning to feel a sense of control returning to his life. It had been a hectic two days, and even more so since the president had left him to play the part of roving fireman. Through the haze, the view was clearing.

Bob Lundgren rarely admitted his faults or bad decisions. It was what pseudo-celebrities had to do, either act confident or move out of the way. There was always some new schmuck looking to take your place. He'd done the rounds as a local news anchor, then moved up to the B-team on prime time, but he'd hit the proverbial glass ceiling. The chosen few were solidly entrenched, and despite a brilliant record as both a live host and an investigative journalist, Bob Lundgren's upward trajectory ground to a halt.

That was until an old friend looking to get some publicity for his first congressional appointment contacted Lundgren and asked for his opinion. To his friend's delight and to Lundgren's surprise the effort had been both enjoyable and painless. Add in the sizable consultancy fee and Lundgren was hooked.

First, he juggled his full-time news gig while helping politicians, businessmen and corporations craft media blitzes that made the Old Spice advertisements look like they were created by amateurs. But when the retainers and bonuses coming in quadrupled the size of the salary from his day job, Lundgren left journalism. He never looked back. For close to ten years, he'd continued to charm clients and hit grand slams for hefty bonuses. He'd become the darling of political hopefuls, charitable organizations and forward-thinking billionaires. He was the big fish and he'd loved it.

But, as is the way with successful overachievers, Lundgren got bored. Every deal felt the same, and every client started to sound like a whiny child. He had enough money to retire comfortably, and he could have walked away from it all. Then the president had called. The two men were rock stars in their respective worlds. They were both good looking and often graced the covers of magazines; they were young and hard-working men.

Lundgren liked Brandon Zimmer and apparently the feeling was mutual. The president had just taken over after his predecessor's abrupt departure and the previous press secretary had just handed in his resignation.

"I'd love for you to come aboard, Bob. I really think together we could accomplish great things," the president had said.

Despite the pay and the prospect of long hours, Lundgren yearned for the challenge. It took him all of ten minutes to say yes. He was in Washington within a week, and started work a day after his relocation.

That seemed liked ages ago, and if you'd asked him a day earlier, Lundgren might have called it a mistake. But now things were becoming clear. What at first seemed like a naive and spur-of-the-moment decision, now coalesced in the press secretary's sharp mind into a cunning, calculated move made by the president.

Zimmer had the world on its heels. Now that the shock had worn off, the teams were settling in for the long game. Leaders who at first had railed at him and his staff over the phone were now calling, not to apologize outright, but to check on the president's progress, respectfully.

The president was right. Something had to be done, and in one swift move he'd called out the entire world. Some might see it as rash and stupid, but Lundgren now saw the brilliance behind the plan. Like a swaggering Teddy Roosevelt shaking his big stick at the world, Zimmer had put everyone on notice. If it could be done with trillion-dollar corporations, why couldn't it be done in politics and diplomacy? If anything, they were all branches protruding from the same tree trunk. Human nature rarely differed. Most people were worried about only one thing - themselves. If the president could flip the status quo like Lincoln, FDR, or maybe even like JFK had...

Bob Lundgren grinned for the first time in two days. Already he was imagining the sweeping headlines, the throngs of supporters waiting to hear Zimmer's every word, and the countries lining up to be at the top of the new pecking order. They could build the new Camelot and enjoy a resurgent love for the White House like the Brits had done with their monarchy.

We could do it, Lundgren thought. *We could go down in history*.

And without another glance towards the ringing phone, Bob Lundgren grabbed a notepad and started writing. He'd tasted the Kool-Aid and he really liked it.

* * *

MARGE HAINES POKED THROUGH THE LAST BOX OF TRAVIS'S things. It had been sitting in the White House residence for months. Brandon had kept it there, waiting for one of Travis's friends to come get his personal effects. She'd just been too busy or at least that's what she'd told herself.

There were pictures including one of Travis with his arm wrapped around Cal, who was wearing Marine Corps fatigues. It had been taken at Camp Lejeune just after Cal received the Navy Cross from the commanding general of the Second Marine Division.

There was also a picture of her and Travis that had been taken either by Top or Gaucho on their trip to Paris. Neither she nor Travis were looking at the camera, but instead they were looking at each other intently. They were seated at a small table with matching glasses of wine between them. Her chest tightened at the memory. It was the first time they'd admitted their feelings to one another. Just steps away from the Louvre, they'd made love in a penthouse Travis arranged for them at the last minute. Their relationship had never been perfect and their busy careers hadn't helped. Marge didn't regret the time spent in their on-again, off-again romance. The only thing she did regret was not telling him how she really felt about him. However, those feelings were buried so deep she was scarcely aware of them.

Staring at the picture of the two of them, she realized that her lifelong need to compartmentalize her life and to succeed in a professional capacity where few women dared to tread possibly had cost her the man she loved. And, she had never told him that she loved him, that she wanted him, and that she might have given it all up just for him. But that was over now. She'd worked long hours to cover her grief, to shield herself from the pain.

But something had happened on the trip to South Carolina. She'd seen Cal, who'd run away in search of answers and now seemed to be on the mend. She'd seen Top and Gaucho, always optimistic, always pressing forward and pulling the rest of them along for the ride. And she'd seen the stoic ones like Daniel and Dr. Higgins, always present and always vigilant. And finally, she'd seen President Brandon Zimmer, the leader of the free world and arguably the most powerful man in the world. And what had he done? He'd put aside the job and joined in the merriment to celebrate Travis's life until the early morning hours in genuine happiness.

Marge felt unsettled, like some part of her perfectly-orchestrated life was coming unhinged. Not in a bad way, but in a way that felt foreign and new to her. She was so used to feeling grounded and sure about her decisions. Even the decision to ask Cal to leave SSI hadn't been difficult. It had been right for both SSI and Cal.

But now things felt different, uncertain, like the ground beneath her feet was shifting slowly and her feet were trying to figure out the pattern of movement.

Marge took one last look at the picture and placed it in her briefcase. There was one more visit to make before heading back to Nashville. The sands continued shifting as she went to say goodbye.

* * *

THE PRESIDENT LOOKED UP FROM HIS READING WHEN Marge came into the small office located next to the master bedroom. She looked tired. He understood. He'd felt the same way after looking through Travis's things.

"How did it go?" he asked.

"It wasn't easy."

"I know."

"The pictures were the hardest."

"Yeah," Brandon answered, remembering that some of the pictures had been of Marge and Travis. "You okay?"

Marge nodded and shifted her briefcase from one hand to the other. She looked like she was thinking and he didn't want to interrupt, but the words came out before he could stop them.

"I miss him."

"Me too," Marge replied, her normally cool eyes welling with tears.

"I'm glad Cal invited us to Charleston. I feel like we got to say goodbye the right way."

"He would have liked it," she said, dabbing a corner of her eye with the back of her hand.

Brandon willed himself not to get emotional. It was past time for that. Instead, he changed the subject.

"Do you head back tonight?"

"I do."

"Do you need a ride?"

Marge started to shake her head and then stopped. Her faced changed, like she'd just come to some realization. Rather than interrupt her thoughts, he waited. Finally her eyes focused on him, her face the steady calm that had earned her the moniker, "The Hammer".

"You've really made a mess of things, haven't you?"

For a moment he was too stunned to reply. Then he noticed the smile on Marge's face.

Brandon chuckled. "I guess I have."

"Do you mind if I give you some unsolicited advice?" Marge asked, taking a step closer, like she was approaching the judge's bench.

"You know I don't."

Marge nodded slowly. "Well, if you ask me, I think it's *about* time you find yourself a new Chief of Staff."

Brandon couldn't help but reciprocate Marge's smile now.

What just moments earlier might have seemed macabre, given that they'd been talking about Travis, now felt like the old days when the SSI team and then Congressman Zimmer could say anything to each other.

"I'd like to put my name in for consideration," Marge said, not taking her eyes off the president. "I'd be happy to provide you with references, if you need them."

She said it in her lawyer voice, the one Brandon knew she'd used for years to tear opposing counsels into pieces. He couldn't help but laugh as he rose from his chair.

"Ms. Haines, I don't think that will be necessary. Consider yourself hired."

They stared at each other for a long spell until Marge held out her hand. Brandon looked down at it, ignored it, and wrapped her in a warm embrace. "It's about time we came to our senses," Brandon whispered as his new Chief of Staff returned the hug. Things were changing now; he could feel it. The pieces of the puzzle were coming together. The team was down a man but it was far from depleted. It was time to come back strong, and this time they would do it together. No man or woman left behind. It felt right; it felt good. How better to take on the world than with the best of friends at your side?

Brandon held Marge at arm's length, thanking the heavens for this wonderful gift. He said, "Things are going to be different now, much different."

Marge grinned and replied, "I'm ready whenever you are, Mr. President."

HAIFA, ISRAEL

3 Hours Earlier

Her bed beckoned as Hannah Krygier tried to focus on the computer screen. She would've liked nothing more than to slide under the sheets and fade away. But she couldn't. Even when she tried to sleep, her mind spun from the toxic mix of anxiety and paranoia that made even the simplest tasks an effort. It was like she was on a roller coaster whose speed kept increasing as it streaked along rickety wooden tracks. She wanted to scream and flail her arms in terror but she couldn't. They were watching her closely. Efraim Perlstein had his goons tailing her around the clock and little effort was made to remain hidden.

It could only mean that Perlstein's plans were progressing. She had no way of knowing if Maya had contacted President Zimmer, and it was too risky to find out. The best she could do was monitor the headlines on America's top media outlets while trying in vain to get a handle on her normal workload. Nothing so far. Either Zimmer was waiting or Maya had been captured.

Her heart sank at the thought. It would be just like Perlstein to withhold that information from her. That was his modus operandi. He would undoubtedly disclose such infor-mation at the worst possible moment, his slippery tongue flicking the barbs at her wounded soul. She wasn't a particu-larly religious woman, but she found herself saying a silent prayer for Maya, that she be guided and protected. It was the best she could do. That thought made her want to laugh at the absurdity of it all. She, Hannah Krygier, sister to the prime minister and a long-term mole for the American government had been relegated to whispering prayers to the darkness.

Krygier bit back the laughter and tried to ignore the futility of the situation. All was not lost. There was always a chance. There had to be. No sooner had the thought embedded in her subconscious when the bell chimed in the front hall signaling a visitor at the gate. Her chest tightened; it could only be one person.

Slowly, she closed her web browser and clicked on the security program linked to her home monitoring system. Three long seconds later, the face of Efraim Perlstein appeared on her screen.

"It's a little late for a house call," she said, trying to sound upbeat.

"Open the gate," came Perlstein's sharp reply.

Hannah clicked the OPEN button on her screen and she heard the gates slide open.

She met him at the front door. He wasn't wearing his customary suit. Instead, he had on a pair of gray linen pants and a dark untucked button-down shirt with some kind of design on it.

"Do you have your passport here?" he asked, pushing past her and walking into the living room.

"I do. Why?"

"Pack a bag. Nothing fancy. Bring a bathing suit or two," he said, his eyes running casually down her frame.

"Is this some kind of joke? I have work to do. My brother…"

"Your brother knows you are leaving with me."

Krygier tried not to let the surprise register on her face. It didn't matter. Perlstein sensed it. Not for the first time she wondered if her brother was in on the whole affair. He was a good man, a man of the people who'd been swept into office on a wave of nationalist support. He'd served his country in the military, and he'd even lost a wife in a Palestinian bombing. She pushed the nagging thought out of her head and asked, "Where are we going?"

"Somewhere warm." Perlstein was pouring himself a drink from the bar. He had an irritating way of making himself at home whenever he came to call. "You have five minutes."

Krygier stood there for a second, wondering if she should push the man for further details. In the end, she felt it was safer to go along with Perlstein. Maybe then she could get a better idea of what was going on. Maybe that was his plan too.

That sliver of hope helped her focus and, four minutes after entering her bedroom, she emerged with a rolling travel bag. Perlstein was pouring himself another drink.

"Ready?" he asked.

"I will be after I get my purse from the kitchen."

He nodded and waved her away.

After gathering her wallet, keys, and passport, Hannah's hand slid over the concealed panel that held her handgun, which she always kept loaded. It was one of five she'd hidden throughout her house. The idea floated within reach; she could do it. She could put the pistol into her purse or even hold it behind her and return to the living room to kill Perlstein. She would have to fight off his men, but her home was well barricaded and she'd been trained by her ex-husband.

But then the thought came again. What if her brother

was conspiring with Perlstein? Any reprieve that killing Perlstein might elicit would only be temporary.

When she emerged from the kitchen the only thing in her hands was her purse. "Shall we?" she said, trying to appear unfazed by being forced out of her home and to a fate yet unknown.

Perlstein could not have cared less. He drained the rest of the drink and motioned for her to leave first. Just as her hand grabbed the doorknob, she felt his hands on her waist. Hannah tensed at this violation and almost spun around until he said, "I just needed to make sure you didn't bring that handgun you have hidden in your kitchen with you. No weapons are allowed on my airplane."

As he frisked her entire body, lingering a bit too long on her inner thighs, Hannah gritted her teeth and looked straight ahead. Then he took the purse from her hands and searched through its contents.

"You can go," he said, handing the bag back to her.

She flashed him an icy glare and opened the door. As she carried her suitcase down the steps, the only thing Hannah could think about was that nothing would please her more than putting a bullet in Efraim Perlstein's head.

WILD DUNES

Island of Palms, South Carolina

AUGUST 28TH, 7:44PM

"I've got him," Neil announced, turning every head in the room.

The tech genius had been on the hunt for Chance Baxter all afternoon. One of The Jefferson Group warriors had said early on that it was nearly impossible for a billionaire to disappear. They had too many responsibilities and too many ties to the world.

They'd gotten the lowdown on their suspect minutes after Neil discovered the identity of the super-yacht, *Nightshade*. Baxter's wealth stretched back many generations. It was stated that his family was one of the oldest families without title. There were no lords or ladies residing in the Baxter family tree. From what Neil could find, the billionaire traced his lineage to the 16th century, during the time of Queen Elizabeth I. The Baxter family often touted the exploits of their most distant relative, an apprentice shipbuilder named William Baxter who was working for Sir Francis Drake, the famous English hero who broke the Spanish Armada in 1588.

It was said that William Baxter concocted the plan and executed the English fire ship attack that sent the Spanish Armada running during the Second Battle of Gravelines which would later lead to its final defeat.

William Baxter was given neither a title of nobility nor land for his part in the English victory but he was given the title of master shipbuilder. Instead, he would stand at Sir Francis Drake's right hand until the vice admiral's death in 1596. It was Drake, known as a privateer to his own people but as a pirate to the Spanish, who introduced Baxter to the slave trade.

After Drake's death, William and his sons expanded their empire until they were a direct competitor of the East India Company in everything ranging from grain to opium. It was also rumored that the English monarchy secretly used the Baxter organization to crush the East India Company when the monopolistic behemoth became too powerful.

From what Neil had told them, the Baxters knew how to stay out of the spotlight. For centuries they'd managed to do so, and within the last hundred years they had paid reparations for their part in the slave trade. On the surface, they seemed like a merchant family who'd toiled against the elite and sometimes with them in order to build a brand that had lasted for almost five hundred years.

There had been the occasional transgression by the younger Baxters, a DUI here or an alleged assault there, but for the rest their records appeared clean. Every Baxter subsidiary was involved in the community, gave money to all British political parties, and donated time, energy and resources to charities around the globe.

On paper, Chance Baxter looked the spitting image of his long-dead ancestor, William Baxter. He graduated from a middle-of-the-road university with a degree in engineering. He'd gone to work for his father after college and spent many years toiling in most of the Baxter subsidiaries. To Cal, the guy who appeared on paper looked like what a billionaire should be. He was a hard worker who'd taken the time to learn the business from the bottom up prior to assuming the reins.

"He's in the Bahamas," Neil said, looking back and forth furtively between computer screens.

"How did you find him?" Cal asked.

Neil sniffed. "You don't want to know."

He was right. Cal didn't want to know. He'd learned a long time ago that the things Neil did to track down money, information and people were rarely legal. Sometimes it made Cal wonder what would happen if a guy with the skills that Neil possessed, but one lacking the moral compass and ethics, were let loose on the world. All the top brass were discussing national security concerns in the face of cyber attacks on American systems. It would not be much of a stretch to then consider the ramifications of people or countries to use cyber technology to either interrupt or disable communications networks or electrical grids.

"Where is he, exactly?" Cal asked.

"He owns an island just north of Grand Bahama. It's called Great Sale Cay and it is about 370 acres. He has a compound and small marina. It's all here in the interview he did with *Inc.* magazine."

Cal looked over Neil's shoulder and skimmed the article. It was a typical "This Is How This Billionaire Lives" piece. There were five pictures, one of Baxter holding up some kind of fish, his smile wide but practiced. *This guy's used to the cameras*, Cal thought.

"Have you gotten anything else from Maya's files?" Cal asked.

"Nada."

It didn't feel right. Why would Hannah Krygier deliver the

random notes to Maya if they couldn't use them? The only thing that had come to fruition was the image of the super-yacht but even that didn't tell them about what they were up against. Hell, Chance Baxter looked like a saint compared to most of the scumbags the men in the room had dealt with over the years. Still, it was the only breadcrumb they had discovered.

"Jonas," Cal said, getting their CEO's attention. "How hard would it be for you to get an introduction to this guy?"

"Are you thinking for you or me?" Jonas Layton asked, humor lacing the words.

"I was thinking we could come up with some story about how you'd like to meet him regarding a project you're working on. You billionaires all know each other, right?"

There were chuckles from the other men and Jonas rolled his eyes.

"It's not that easy, Cal. I don't even know the guy."

"But you could come up with something?"

Jonas thought about it for a moment and then nodded. "Let me get in touch with one of my assistants in charge of setting up that sort of introduction."

Cal nodded and turned back to Neil.

"Get me everything you can on that island and whatever else Baxter owns in the area."

"Okay. What about his yachts?"

"What do you mean?"

"Do you want to know where his yachts are too?"

"How many yachts does he have?" Cal asked, incredulously.

Neil counted from a list on his screen.

"Twenty-three."

Trent whistled. "Maybe Jonas should let me have the introduction."

Cal ignored him.

"Yes, get me the information on all his assets in and around the Bahamas."

"That could take some time. He's got property scattered under a plethora of different entities," Neil said.

"Do your best."

Neil clicked his teeth together and got back to work.

Cal decided that things were well in hand for the moment. He needed time to think, to step back and examine the pieces of the puzzle. He figured a walk would do him some good, so he told the others where he was going and he stepped outside.

When he got to the street, a car was just pulling up to the end of the cul-de-sac. The driver's window rolled down revealing Todd Dunn.

"You got a minute?" Dunn asked.

"Sure. What's up?"

"Did you hear about Marge?"

"She texted me. Congrats on the pay raise. You cool with it?" Cal asked.

Dunn shrugged. "She's been dropping me subtle hints for months. I figured it might happen."

People who didn't know Todd Dunn, whose official title had been Head of Internal Security at SSI for years, thought that the former Ranger was just another muscle-bound meat-head. Cal and his friends knew better. Since he'd arrived at SSI, first under Travis and then under Marge Haines, Dunn had been much more than a security guard. He knew every secret and protected it with the intensity of a Doberman. He was also much smarter than he ever let on. The MBA he'd earned while going to school after hours was only one such indication of his intelligence. In short, Cal knew Dunn was more than capable of running SSI.

"If it means anything to you, I think you're the right man

for the job," Cal said. He was more than happy that Dunn was taking over the Stokes' family business.

"Thanks."

"You heading back tonight?"

"Yeah, but I've got something for you. It's in the back."

Dunn stepped out of the small SUV and popped open the rear hatch. Cal heard what sounded like metal on metal and then he saw Dunn reach into the back. He pulled something out and set it on the ground.

"Go ahead," Dunn said to the ground.

Cal cocked an eyebrow in confusion. A second later a chocolate brown dog with white- ticked legs walked around the car. Cal didn't know a thing about dogs but he knew she was just a puppy. Then, to Cal's astonishment the dog took a seat and stared directly in his eyes, waiting for his command.

"You got a dog?" Cal asked.

"She's not mine."

"What breed is she?"

"She's a German Shorthaired Pointer," Dunn said.

The dog hadn't moved. It was still gazing intently at Cal.

"And she belongs to —?"

Dunn hesitated and then said, "Travis had an order in with a breeder up in Indiana. I didn't know about it until the guys called SSI requesting final payment."

Cal gulped. The dog, as if sensing his unease, held out a paw. Cal bent down to get a better look at the beautiful pointer and he took the extended paw. The dog licked his hand once and then looked up at him again. There was an ease there, like an older dog trapped in a puppy's body. Cal wondered if all dogs were that brilliant and well-behaved, or if Dunn had trained her that way. He stroked her head, feeling the velvety fur under his fingers. It was just the kind of dog Travis would want. Trav loved to hunt, and he'd always wanted a bird dog. Cal pictured his cousin sitting by a fire, the dog curled up at his feet while he sipped a glass of Jack Daniels, his belly full of whatever they'd got that day. He gulped again, his newfound emotions bubbling to the surface.

"What are you going to do with her?" he asked.

"Travis left everything to you."

It took Cal a couple beats to realize what Dunn was saying.

"You want *me* to take her?" But even as he asked the question and looked into the dog's eyes, Cal knew he would. Still stunned he continued, "What did you name her?"

"I didn't. Travis did."

Cal's mouth felt dry. He couldn't take his eyes off the dog.

"What's her name, Dunn?"

After a moment, Dunn said, "Liberty. He named her Liberty."

Cal stared at the dog as if it might bring him closer to understanding his cousin's death. There was no answer there but there was something else. What was it? He realized it a split second later. The dog was a piece of Travis, like an extension of his cousin's life, and a treasure left behind that Travis knew Cal needed.

Cal smiled and the dog cocked its head as if studying him. This time she moved in close, slithering in under his arm, leaning against him like she needed his body heat. Cal stroked her back and said, "Liberty; I like that."

The only response he got back from the dog was a soft happy whine and the wag of her tail.

GREAT SALE CAY

The Bahamas

AUGUST 28TH, 8:31PM

"Thank you for the update, Doctor. I hope I did not keep you too long." Chance Baxter wiped his mouth before refolding the cloth napkin, setting it on the table.

"I am happy to answer any questions you might have, Mr. Baxter," Dr. Aviel Nahas replied. He could feel the white wine going to his head. There was still work do be done that night, but part of him wanted to stay and talk to his host. "If I may say, Mr. Baxter, it has been a pleasure to work with someone who not only cares for my work, but also has gone to such extremes to ensure I am well taken care of. The laboratory alone must have cost…"

"Do not worry about the cost, Doctor. Your research and development are well worth the modest investment. Perhaps once we have concluded this particular project we can talk about your future with us."

"I would like that very much, Mr. Baxter. Thank you."

Baxter smiled and rose from the table. "Now, if you will

excuse me, there are certain matters that I must attend to. Please let me know if there is anything you need."

He was gone from the room before Dr. Nahas could properly stand up from his chair. The Israeli inventor watched his new benefactor depart. He was in awe of the man really. How could he not be? Baxter genuinely cared about Nahas's work and had even proposed his own ideas in the most diplomatic way possible. He listened. Nahas had never worked for such a man. One word came to mind when he tried to describe the billionaire - benevolent.

It was easy to try to please such a man, a man whose family had done such great things over the centuries. Nahas had known some of the Baxter family history, but his host had filled in the details. There was no bravado in Baxter's retelling only the fond pride a good man has for his ancestors.

The Israeli smiled at the thought. He felt fortunate to be working for a man like Baxter. Nahas hoped that boded well for his own future within the Baxter organization, as well as for the success of his current undertaking.

* * *

CHANCE BAXTER WAS PLEASED. NOT ONLY WAS DR. NAHAS ahead of schedule, but also he'd improved on his concept. Baxter watched as the updated software and schematics left his outbox and sped out to the intended recipients. He'd meant every word he'd uttered to Nahas. It was a pleasure to work with an innovator whose mind knew no bounds. Given the right tools, time, and resources, Nahas could become one of his greatest assets.

After he'd initially apologized for the abrupt departure from Israel, Baxter soothed Nahas with promises of unlimited funding. But it was what he'd uncovered in their first conversation that really made all the difference. It became painfully obvious to Baxter that Nahas wanted one thing - recognition. He might not know the breadth of what he was building until the very end, if at all, but Baxter would wrap him in praise and boost the inventor's self-worth until Nahas was ready to burst with well-earned pride.

It was one of the many ways Chance Baxter had secured his company for the modern age. He had an eye for talent and a gift for solemn flattery. Men like Nahas melted under the praise of men like Baxter. It remained to be seen whether Nahas would grasp the value of their mission but that could wait. He didn't have to know the whole picture to complete his task. After all, compartmentalization was the way of the world now. It was "need to know," as they say in the movies.

When the message signaling the successful transmission appeared on his screen, Chance Baxter closed the browser and made his way downstairs. His staff said the helicopter had just left. A new shipment had been delivered – ah, a new traitor to enjoy. He'd read the report, and the man knew little. He was a simple saboteur who'd been caught red-handed. It might have been easier for the vessel's captain to dispose of the man, but Baxter's instructions had been clear.

Baxter smiled when he saw the sealed white cooler at the entrance to the hallway leading to his secret chamber. His house manager, George, was standing next to the package, ever the dutiful employee.

"Would you like help pushing the cooler, Mr. Baxter?"

"Thank you, George, but I think I can manage."

George nodded and left the entryway.

Less than a minute later, Baxter was inside his soundproof room. He took his time changing, this time opting to go with a set of swim trunks and no shirt. It was messy work and he did hate to spoil good clothing.

When he'd finished depositing his dinner clothes in the plastic bag George had left on top of the locked cooler,

Baxter carefully entered the combinations for the two locks on the side of the container. The pressure seal popped open with very little effort and Baxter was greeted with the familiar smell of fear. It might have been repugnant to most but the odor aroused Baxter's senses. His arousal increased all the more when he looked into the cooler and saw the frightened eyes of his newest guest. The man was strapped to the bottom and his nose and mouth were covered with a clear mask with tubes winding down to the twin oxygen tanks at the man's side.

Baxter lifted the mask from the man's face.

"What are you...?"

Baxter put a finger to his own mouth and said, "Shh. We don't want to wake the sharks yet."

* * *

OFF THE COAST OF CABO SAN LUCAS, MEXICO - 9:01PM

As the chief steward of the mega-yacht, *Suprema*, it was Jeanette Locke's job to keep the guests happy. She was very good at her job or she would have been fired long ago. Catering to the upper crust of society took both patience and an eye for detail. It also required utmost discretion, which her current captain harped on regularly.

"Our guests pay for our silence," he would say. "Let us prove to them the crew of *Suprema* understands that need."

But it wasn't the guests that had Jeanette on edge or her never-ending duties as chief steward. What concerned Jeanette most was what was happening in the bowels of the yacht. To the untrained eye, the new crew members appeared to be your run-of-the mill yacht enthusiasts, but there was something about them that only amplified Jeanette's unease. It appeared there were now two separate crews on the yacht ;

one crew cared for the guests and the other crew's mission was yet unknown. She was aware of them working odd hours in the secure cargo hold, and their mission was off limits to even the captain of the yacht.

She'd already relayed this information to her superiors in London, despite the captain's stranglehold on communication with the outside world. But it had been easy for Jeanette. As chief steward she required access to ship-to-shore communications. It was her job to order all items that her rich guests desired or required.

The message had been encoded like she'd been instructed. Nobody would know that she'd just reported the sighting of "unusual activity" to MI6. She only wished that it could have been sent earlier. However, it had taken an unusual request for a rare brand of tequila from their thirty-something millionaire guest to allow the transmission.

As Jeanette closed the door to the master cabin, the captain's voice came over her earpiece. "Jeanette, could you please come to the bridge?"

"On my way, captain," she replied, hurrying to the nearest staircase. Little did she know that she'd just performed her final act as yacht chief steward.

OFF THE COAST OF CABO SAN LUCAS, MEXICO

August 28th, 9:17pm

The yacht was anchored so when Jeanette entered the dimly lit bridge of *Suprema* the only person on watch was the captain. He was standing behind the wheel, hands at 10 and 2 like he was about to take her underway.

"You wanted to see me, Captain?" Jeanette asked.

His head turned slowly. He was the youngest captain she'd ever worked for. He was possibly in his mid forties. The heavily-bearded master of the vessel rarely yelled and never had to ask his employees twice to complete his orders. His eyes said far more than any curse he could have uttered.

As Jeanette waited for a response, she noted that the captain's eyes had softened, looking wistful.

"How are our guests?" he asked absentmindedly.

"Preparing for tonight's festivities, Captain."

Their primary charter guest had requested a Mexican themed fiesta for their last night aboard the yacht. That meant Jeanette had to obtain multiple bottles of tequila and enough quesadillas to soak up some of the day's alcohol.

"Good," the captain said. "There's been another request."

Jeanette flashed a knowing smile. "Trying to milk every last minute of their charter, are they?"

The captain nodded, but he didn't return the smile. Jeanette stared at him, waiting.

Finally, his hand slipped into his tunic. Jeanette's body tensed. When the hand emerged again it held a folded piece of paper.

"Here's the list," the captain said, handing her the paper.

Jeanette unfolded the sheet and read the list. They all looked like items currently stocked in the ship's galley, nothing out of the ordinary. There was an address under the list, not located in Mexico, but instead in the Bahamas. She almost looked up in confusion, but then she read the the final two words at the bottom of the page.

They know.

Jeanette's breath caught as fear and panic swam over her.

"I would commit the list to memory, just in case," the captain was saying even as Jeanette's heart thudded in her chest. "I suggest you have Edison take you to shore now. The man at that address will assist you in obtaining the more obscure items."

Jeanette nodded, her eyes wide. The captain's eyes glanced in the direction of the digital display. It took a second for her to realize what he was trying to convey. *The cameras,* she thought. There were cameras all over the yacht. While that wasn't uncommon, she'd always suspected that the video being taken on *Suprema* was being watched in some place other than the multi million-dollar craft.

She did her best to look unconcerned even as her stomach did somersaults. Then it hit her. If the captain knew, didn't that mean that he was working for MI6, as well? No one had told her that the captain was in on the surveillance, but then again, why would they? And if he stayed, didn't that mean that he would be caught? Maybe he had a contingency plan for that, or at least, that's what she told herself as she said goodbye to the captain, who had already turned his attention to the wheel.

* * *

THERE WAS A LEAK. THAT'S WHAT THE MESSAGE HAD SAID. Carefully inserted into the package of Toblerone chocolate was a thin piece of flash paper. The decoded message, for security reasons, had been brief and to the point.

Leak confirmed. Two compromised. Good luck.

Montgomery Weir had been captain of *Suprema* for five years. He'd worked for MI6 for half of that time. The secret intelligence organization initially recruited him because of the growing number of wealthy Arabs *Suprema* hosted. As a former sailor and a devout British citizen, Weir had the perfect cover. Then the order had come suggesting that he put his name in for some undertaking that the billionaire Chance Baxter was organizing. The assignment was all very hush-hush. Weir was approved only after providing his credentials and after sitting through no less than eight interviews.

Initially, it seemed like more of a patriotic fraternity. The yacht captains, many of whom already knew one another, either from their time in the British Navy or from their yachting days, gathered twice a year at Baxter's London headquarters. There they were treated like a brotherhood, and much was discussed about the future of the British empire. They lamented the loss of Hong Kong and India. Over endless cocktails, they shared the hope that one day their country might regain its rightful place in the world.

What had seemed like nostalgic camaraderie took a serious turn. Baxter had a plan to consolidate many of the world's private yachts under his umbrella. With the help of their captains, he was able to accomplish this feat. So,in just under three years, Chance Baxter had control of some of the world's finest private vessels. In short, he'd bought his own private navy comprised of 28 super-yachts.

That, in and of itself, wasn't the problem. Until a few weeks ago, Weir had had little to report. However, then the team of engineers had arrived on his command and the retrofit had begun. And then, just before leaving port to pick up their guests, a large shipment was loaded onto *Suprema*.

He was never given a reason, just the order to comply with the engineers instructions. Then once the cargo was loaded into the modified hold a small team was left behind to tend to it. Captain Weir couldn't be sure, but an educated guess marked the six-man team as former military, possibly special operations. The team volunteered to assist his crew. However, they reminded Weir of Soviet political officers who had boarded Soviet ships to ensure the Communist ideals were being met.

Fortunately, he'd saved Jeanette. The address on the sheet he'd given her was an MI6 safe house. They knew she was coming, and both a fake passport and plane ticket were waiting at the Los Cabos International Airport. Weir hoped she would make it. At least he'd given her a fighting chance.

As for him, he didn't know how much time he had. They hadn't received orders from Baxter in twenty-four hours. Maybe that was part of the master plan or maybe they were waiting until all MI6 agents were caught. Weir wondered how many agents there were. Were their orders the same as his, to watch and wait?

They'd been clear during his training. If the word ever came that his mission was compromised, he was on his own. As the captain of the craft, he did not have the protection that its chief steward had. It hadn't seemed like much of a risk at the time, but now the knowledge of being disavowed weighed heavily on Weir like a lead life jacket.

It would seem odd if he went ashore. What business could he have in Cabo San Lucas? A yacht captain's place was on his yacht.

Weir let go of the wheel and radioed for his first mate. The man appeared minutes later, a cup of coffee in his hand.

"I thought you might like some, Captain," the young man said. He was a good lad, always patient with the crew and wise beyond his years.

"I've already had some. Thank you."

"Is there anything I should know, sir?"

"All's quiet," the captain replied. "I sent Jeanette ashore with Edison."

"Another bottle of tequila for our young guest?" the first mate asked, grinning.

"Something like that. I told her to get a room at the usual hotel if it gets too late. We can always send someone to fetch her in the morning." If the man was one of Baxter's spies, he was very good. He showed no signs of worry over the chief steward's absence. "I'll be up to relieve you at two," he said, with a nod.

"Good night, Captain."

"Good night."

CAPTAIN MONTGOMERY WEIR STAYED IN HIS STATEROOM for thirty minutes. It was long enough to hear that Jeanette had made it safely to shore. It also gave him ample time to retrieve a backpack from his private safe. With a decisive grunt, he strapped it over one shoulder and made his way aft. He could feel the thumping of the music as he got closer. The party overhead must be in full swing. No doubt the guests were dancing on top of the tables like kids on spring break.

But he wasn't going to visit the guests, and when he got to the stairs leading up to the helipad he passed that too. When he got to his destination, he knocked on the heavy metal door. A moment later, one of the six men guarding the cargo opened the door.

"Yes, Captain?" the man asked politely.

"The chef had some leftovers from the party. I was on my way to bed and thought I'd bring them by." He motioned to the pack on his shoulder.

The man put out a hand to take the bag but Weir didn't move.

"There's also been word. Didn't you get the message?"

The man's face twisted in confusion.

"There's been no message."

"Damn. They said something like this might happen. Some issue with communications. May I come in? You can eat while I tell you what I know."

Weir held his breath as the man mulled it over. The captain knew what he was thinking. On the one hand, the cargo cell was not supposed to talk to the captain about the operation without explicit word from London. But, on the other hand, if there was word, shouldn't they listen to what the captain had to say? After all, he was one person against six of them.

Finally, the man nodded and opened the door.

Weir stepped inside and took in the modified space. Three of the men were stretched out on cots chatting. The talk ceased when they saw him. Two more men were staring at computer screens that had wires running into the large capsule taking up the bulk of the space.

"The captain says he has a message," the man behind him reported.

One of the men at the computers turned.

"How can I help you, Captain?"

Weir saw annoyance in the man's eyes. He was in their domain.

Weir stepped forward, shifting the pack on his shoulder. It felt heavy now, like someone had added a fifty-pound plate on his way below deck.

"Here," he said, handing the pack to the man in charge.

"What is it?" the man asked, already beginning to open the zipper.

Six, five, four... Weir thought.

"A gift," Weir said, all nervousness gone now. He could feel the ominous power of whatever sat inside the mounted capsule. It was the last resort but he was ready. He'd done his patriotic duty. Maybe this would put Baxter on his heels. Maybe...

Three, two, one.

The explosives detonated at the precise moment when the man had opened the main compartment. They hadn't explained to Weir exactly what it was, but he had seen the video. This "gift" acted no differently. The explosives ripped *Suprema* in half and then like a supernova the explosion tore outward engulfing the entire vessel in fire. *Suprema*, its obliterated crew and guests all hit the bottom of the ocean two minutes later.

FREEPORT, BAHAMAS

August 29th, 9:02am

I t was pretty convenient having a company plane. After the decision was made to contact Chance Baxter, The Jefferson Group had chartered a flight to the Bahamas. They knew he was there and the best thing to do was get close. Besides, the TJG pilots said there was a storm coming in, possibly turning into a hurricane. Ergo, they had no time to wait.

Cal stroked his new puppy's neck as they touched down in Freeport. Other than a quick pit stop in Miami, the newest member of the team, Liberty, had been calm and quiet. She snuggled against Cal's leg during most of the flight, perfectly content with just being near him.

"Cal, the authorities are heading over to check our passports," Benny said, opening the door and letting in the warm Bahamian air.

"You heard the man, everybody up," barked Trent, stretching, as much as the cabin would allow. He yawned deeply and was the first to the door when the man in the airport uniform arrived.

Cal followed Trent out of the plane, holding Liberty on a

short leash. She was quick to find a spot to do her business, and after a glance down the runway as another private jet landed, she hustled back to his side.

By that time Jonas, Gaucho, Daniel and Neil had deplaned and were showing their passports to the airport authority who'd joined them and was conversing casually. He gave them each one last cursory glance and then walked over to take Cal's passport.

"Welcome to the Bahamas, Mr. Stokes," the man said after examining the passport. "Are there more visitors on board?" he asked, pointing to the aircraft.

"The crew and one more," Cal answered.

The man nodded and made his way up the ladder. Maya was still in there gathering her things. She handed over the fake passport and tried to act like nothing was amiss. The man didn't notice and moved on to the pilots.

When Maya finally made her way outside, Cal waved her over.

"Everything okay?" he asked.

"Why shouldn't it be?" she replied, scanning the area.

"You were pretty quiet on the flight down."

She shrugged. "I'd like to get this over with."

Something had changed in the woman after they'd made the decision to confront Baxter. It was as if Maya, in an attempt to put her training to good use, was dealing with her grief. Cal understood that feeling and hoped they would find what they needed. He knew it wouldn't be easy but maybe they'd get lucky.

"Hey, here comes our ride," Trent said, pointing to a shiny stretch limo rumbling down the tarmac. It parked next to them and a thin black man stepped out.

"Mr. Layton?" he asked the small crowd.

Jonas raised a hand. "That's me."

The driver gave a half bow. "Mr. Baxter's compliments, sir. May I take your bags?"

"I think we can throw them in ourselves," Jonas answered as he made his way to the open trunk.

They all tossed their overnight bags in the back and hopped in. It was a short ride over to the private helipad on the edge of the airport. They had time for a complimentary snack and soda on the way over.

The driver opened the door and let them out.

"Gentlemen and lady, the first helicopter will be here in thirty minutes. If you would like to go to the lounge and have a drink, everything is paid for."

They already knew from the message from Jonas's assistant that they'd be taking two helicopters off the main island and from there to Great Sale Cay. Boats would've taken longer and there was no runway on the private island. In fact, Baxter had insisted on sending his own aircraft to fetch them.

I guess that's what fellow billionaires do for one another, Cal had thought as he'd packed his bag. There hadn't been much time to speak with Diane after Maya's dramatic entrance the day before. She had left quietly after giving him a lingering hug and a kiss on the cheek.

"Be careful, okay?" she'd said.

He'd promised he would. After all, how much trouble could they get into on a tiny island in the Bahamas?

Two hours later, the whole TJG crew was safely on Great Sale Cay. They'd been met by a team of Baxter's household staff who'd shuttled them to the main house in open-topped jeeps. The island was barely developed and the roads were rife with potholes. The bumpy ride wasn't long though and soon they'd entered Chance Baxter's massive mansion.

Cal estimated that the place must be close to 20,000

square feet. He wondered how they'd gotten all the supplies over from either the U.S. or Freeport. The construction must have cost a fortune.

"Mr. Layton, I am George, the house manager. Mr. Baxter has provided the east wing for you and your staff. Will you follow me please?"

They followed George through the colonial hallways and under the mighty pillars holding up massive ceilings.

"Now, I could definitely get used to this place," Trent whispered in his ear.

Cal nodded. Baxter definitely knew how to live. Cal stopped counting after the twelfth house staff member he'd seen shuttling down side halls or half bowing to them as they passed. The place really was massive and Cal amended his initial estimate. Maybe the place was double the size. He wondered if there was an underground component.

When they arrived in the east wing, George first ushered in Jonas. As the guest of honor, he would have the largest bedroom. The rest of them would share rooms. Cal and Daniel left their bags in their room and followed Trent as he and Gaucho scoped out their room.

"Pretty nice," Gaucho said, adding a low whistle.

"How come we don't live like this, Cal?" Trent joked, flopping down on one of the two king size beds in the room.

"Don't get started," Gaucho said with a grin.

After everyone had stowed their luggage in their respective rooms, George once again escorted them, but this time into an enormous living area. One wall had a floor-to-ceiling glass window and the view of the ocean was breathtaking. Cal could only imagine what it looked like in the morning as the sun was peaking over the horizon.

Two women dressed in casual servant attire served mimosas and light appetizers. It wasn't yet noon, but everyone, with the exception of Daniel accepted the alcoholic beverages. There was something about being in the middle of a lion's den that caused some uneasiness, although they were also struck by the magnificence of their surroundings. Even Maya looked a bit awestruck. Cal only wished that they could've smuggled in a few weapons, just in case. They didn't know if Baxter was involved personally but the Marine in Cal never liked to walk into a situation unprepared. At the moment he felt a bit naked without his trusty sidearm. He glanced at Daniel to see if he felt the same but the sniper only nodded and gave him a thin smile as if to say, "I'm ready."

That was Daniel, always ready. Cal breathed a little easier knowing that. He'd often thought of Daniel as his lucky rabbit's foot, but then he realized that Daniel had been there when Travis died. Maybe not so lucky.

Cal's thoughts were interrupted when the large double doors at the far end of the room opened, and a tall man wearing a loose-fitting button down-shirt and a pair of swim trunks walked in.

"I'm sorry to keep you waiting," Baxter said, extending his hand to Layton, his official guest.

"It's a pleasure to meet you, Mr. Baxter. Thank you for seeing me on such short notice."

"Not a problem at all, and please, call me Chance."

There was a knowing look exchanged as if each had just passed muster.

"Chance, this is my trusty staff all here to ensure I don't make a stupid decision and buy something I can't afford."

They all chuckled dutifully including Baxter, who said, "If your reputation has any bearing on a future purchase, I am sure it is I who should be concerned."

Jonas laughed at that and the two men shuffled into a quiet corner to discuss whatever it was that billionaires discussed.

"What do you think?" Cal asked Daniel.

"He seems okay, for now."

"Yeah, I wonder if we'll have a chance to look around."

Daniel shrugged as he popped another conch fritter in his mouth.

* * *

HANNAH KRYGIER STRETCHED HER TIRED MUSCLES. Normally, she would've gone to the gym or taken a jog to shake off the cobwebs from the Transatlantic flight but her traveling companion was not letting her out of his sight. They'd even shared a bedroom in the penthouse suite in Freeport.

Luckily, Perlstein hadn't made a pass at her again and he had contented himself with the liquor on the side table. He'd drunk himself into a stupor the previous night but if Hannah had any compulsion to take advantage of the situation by stabbing him in the throat like she wanted, she only had to glance at the two security personnel sitting in the corner to squash that delicious thought.

It was morning now and even though the clock said she'd slept for six hours, it felt more like six minutes. Her mind still whirled as it had since they'd left Israel. She didn't even know where they were headed until they touched down and she'd read the sign on the side of the airport.

Perlstein was once again hitting the booze and he held his second screwdriver of the morning as he chatted away on his phone. He was just out of earshot but Hannah kept glancing at him anyway. She needed a leg up, a stroke of luck or a thorn in Perlstein's side.

She huffed in frustration and went back to her reading. There were numerous American magazines stacked neatly on the coffee table, and she'd pretended to be reading them since waking. It was the only thing she could do since the television had been commandeered by the security guards. So, she watched cautiously out of the corner of her eye as she tried to listen in on Perlstein's conversation.

Hannah didn't catch much but she had heard something about a helicopter ride in an hour. She wondered where they were going and whether she'd ever see Israel again.

* * *

BAXTER SAID GOODBYE TO HIS GUEST AND RETURNED TO HIS office. It had been an interesting and spirited conversation with the man the rich knew as "The Fortuneteller." Baxter had never met Jonas Layton before and, after reading the man's dossier, he had expected a bookish nerd who had a laptop strapped to his hip. He'd been pleasantly surprised at finding the exact opposite.

Layton was funny and smart, but he also seemed more grounded than the many other wealthy acquaintances Baxter had met over the years. Most were either fake in their kindness or mute to the point of being rude.

But the timing was strange. Then again, what was timing to a man who was worth billions? Men of their ilk could do pretty much anything they wanted, anytime they wanted. Take the Baxter home on Great Sale Cay, for example. The deserted isle had gone undeveloped since the Earth had spewed forth its foundation a millennium before. Everyone had said he was crazy when he'd snatched it up for a steal. They said he couldn't build on it due to the insane costs involved.

But Baxter had plans for the island. He wanted it to not only be his home away from home, but also his fortress, his secret lair where no unbidden guests could enter. He had plans to build long piers on either end of the island and a port that could accommodate his largest creations. At one time, he'd envisioned having a shipwright station on the island but reconsidered. Too many visitors. Too many workers.

No, he wanted and needed his privacy. After all, if he was going to see his home country resume its rightful place in the world pecking order, he had to have an outpost halfway around the world from which he could command his navy.

He smiled as he walked, the familiar allure of glory and national pride filling him with warmth and gratitude for what his ancestors had done. They were proud stewards of their great nation, and it had all come down to him to carry on their aspirations. He would raise the banner once again.

But first there was work to do. He had more guests arriving within the hour. Better to get them on solid land before the storm hit. Baxter smirked at the irony. The storm before the storm. Was it truly fate?

If only he'd known the fate of his faithful *Suprema* crew off the coast of Mexico, his smile might not have been so wide.

GREAT SALE CAY

The Bahamas

AUGUST 29TH, 12:44PM

It took every ounce of self control the billionaire had not to scream. The helicopter with Efraim Perlstein had just arrived. The second group of guests were getting settled when George had delivered the sealed envelope the helicopter pilot had brought with him. It was an antiquated and slow way of receiving information, but who knew what the world's intelligence agencies could see or hear?

Actually, Baxter knew quite well what capabilities the intelligence agencies possessed. He received, on an annual basis, a rundown from his friends at MI6. He was quite fortunate to have such friends. It hadn't hurt in the financial department either. A subtle tip dropped here and there had netted him many millions over the years. If only the normal citizenry knew what intelligence arms of major powers were truly capable of.

But that wasn't what had Baxter vexed at that very moment. He was reading the concise report from his radio station in Freeport.

Suprema sunk. Unknown explosion last night. More soon.

Suprema. That was Weir's yacht. Weir, the spy. His plant at MI6 had confirmed Weir and the chief steward were spying on him. On him! As if anyone could stop him.

He gritted his teeth and tried to think of some order to send back with the pilot. They'd decentralized some of the operation, but the final order always was his, and his alone. Not one deviation could happen without his approval. He was the architect.

His foot tapped as he tried to think of some way to salvage what that bastard Weir had somehow managed to accomplish. He didn't have confirmation, yet he knew in his soul that's what had happened.

How many more saboteurs were out there? His man at MI6 had confirmed that Weir and his chief steward were the last two. Could there be more he didn't know about? That thought prickled his brain as he urged his mind to refocus. It was what he got paid for, to find the solution despite the problems.

Finally, the words came to him. He wrote:

Message all vessels. You will take safe anchor and wait until further word.

He resealed the envelope and pressed a buzzer on his desk that rang for George. His attendant appeared a moment later and took the envelope from Baxter.

"When would you like to see your new guests, Mr. Baxter?"

Baxter almost screamed at the man. He wanted to. He really did. But that wasn't his way. George would know something was amiss, and the last thing he needed was for the household staff gossiping about their master's explosive mood.

He took a deep breath and said, "Tell them I'll be with them in fifteen minutes."

George did his usual half bow and said, "Very good, sir."

"Oh, and George, make sure our various groups do not intermingle. Am I understood?"

"Yes, Mr. Baxter. Your new guests are in the far wing in the lowest level."

"Good. Thank you, George."

Another half bow and George was gone.

Baxter exhaled and thanked his foresight and vision to create a headquarters that not only spanned close to 40,000 square feet above ground, but also had underground levels that almost rivaled those above. The last thing he needed was for his potential customers to run into Perlstein and the ever-engaging Hannah Krygier.

Baxter had never met the woman but he'd heard plenty about her from Perlstein. The man could be a real pervert and had told Baxter, who assumed he was now Chance's close friend, what a catch Krygier might be. The billionaire hadn't known whether the Israeli was bragging or suggesting he make a pass. The way Perlstein described her character fascinated Baxter, who lived to meet outliers since he lived hidden among the boring masses.

He knew he was a snob in his own way and it was one of the reasons he had invited a man like Jonas Layton into his house. Interesting always beat mundane. Layton was a legend even though he wasn't yet forty years of age.

If what Perlstein had said in his emails was true, Krygier might be just as interesting, if not more. She didn't have billions, and she wasn't known outside the closest circles in Israel, but she was the Israeli prime minister's sister, and she was the only woman the openly sexist Perlstein had trusted with their plot.

So, while part of his psyche raged over the loss of *Suprema*, the rest of him was already moving on. It was what you had to do to succeed. It was why most people would never attain the level of success that Baxter and his ancestors had. You had to wear blinders, ignore the pot shots, and just keep moving forward.

Baxter smiled as he readied himself for another performance.

* * *

HANNAH STOOD WHEN THE DOOR OPENED. PERLSTEIN hadn't even knocked before entering and she was about to throw him a scowl when the stranger entered.

"Ms. Krygier, I'm sorry to barge in. You know how impulsive our friend Efraim can be."

The man gave her a wink and grin. She couldn't help but return his smile.

"My name is Baxter, Ms. Krygier. Chance Baxter, at your service."

Hannah shook the man's hand. It was strong and warm. Perlstein hadn't told her who their host was, but now that she saw him, it was obvious he was the man of the house.

"It is a pleasure to meet you, Mr. Baxter."

Baxter didn't do anything as forward as kissing her hand or, God forbid, give her an embrace with a kiss on each cheek, but he did squeeze her hand and give a glance toward the back of Efraim Perlstein, who was once again availing himself of the open bar.

Hannah didn't know what to think of the look. Was this Baxter teasing her, or was he someone who could become an ally? He didn't look gay, yet he didn't look at her like she was some sort of prize or worse a piece of meat. She'd found that many successful men did. Baxter did not and she appreciated that. Maybe it was because of what she'd been through in the preceding days, or maybe it was because her senses were dulled from the stress and lack of sleep, but she was drawn to…to something. What was it? Suddenly it hit her, what she saw in the man's eyes and sensed in his every word, something she hadn't thought possible. For the first time in days she felt hope.

"Ms. Krygier, I was hoping to steal Efraim for a few minutes. Would that be alright?" Baxter asked.

"Only if you promise to steal him forever," she answered with a wink.

Baxter laughed deeply. Perlstein turned and stared at her with his bored displeasure.

"I'm sorry, Efraim," Hannah offered to her fellow country-man. Then she turned back to Baxter. "Of course, you may take him. Where would you like me to go?"

"George is just outside the door. He will escort you to my office."

Hannah smiled and walked to the door. George was waiting and she followed him deeper into Baxter's complex.

* * *

"You were right about how beautiful she is," Baxter mused, grabbing himself a glass of orange juice from the bar. "Why did you bring her?"

"I don't trust her," Perlstein growled. He punctuated the comment by guzzling the rest of the whiskey in his glass.

"Are you saying you made a mistake bringing her in?"

"I did not say that."

"And did you not tell me that having her in on our little operation would only benefit us?" There was an edge to

Baxter's tone now and Perlstein finally picked up on it like a child who'd just realized he'd talked back to his father.

"She is my responsibility."

"Yes."

"And I will take care of her."

"Please, Efraim, do tell me what you intend to do. This is my house after all and anything that happens under my roof will eventually come to my attention."

Baxter looked up at the air vent and made sure Perlstein knew what he was looking at. There were no cameras but the cocky Jew didn't need to know that.

"I get your point. I apologize," Perlstein said curtly.

Baxter smiled as if the disagreement had never happened.

"Now, I have some rather disturbing news," Baxter said, although he still wore a smile.

"What is it?"

"We've lost one of our yachts."

"Which one?"

"*Suprema*."

Perlstein inhaled. "How did it happen?"

"We don't know yet. It could have been an accident, or there may have been a malfunction with the cargo.

It was an obvious jab at Dr. Nahas and, by extension, Perlstein himself. The Israeli's chest puffed out just perceptibly.

"You are the one who has Nahas as a guest, not I. Was it not one of your vessels piloted by your crew that has now, how did you put it?"

"It blew up," Baxter answered, sipping his juice.

"It blew up?"

Baxter nodded.

There was a tense thirty seconds where neither man said a word. They were the co-architects of the bold plot and the only ones who knew their halves of the plan. Baxter wasn't going to tell Perlstein that he'd known about Captain Weir and his accomplice, and that maybe they had something to do with the explosion. Better to leave that part out because Perlstein had a nasty way of holding grudges, as well as an annoying way of bringing up past mistakes at the most inopportune times.

The man was used to getting his way in Israel, but that was where his reach stopped. He needed Chance Baxter and the vast network that he and his corporation commanded. No, Baxter would not admit anything to Perlstein. Better to let him come up with his own conclusions.

"Have you talked to Nahas?" Perlstein asked.

"I have not."

"Would you like me to speak with him?"

"That would not be wise."

Perlstein bristled again. "I think you forget that it was I who brought Dr. Nahas to you. Without him and his research…"

"Neither of us would be here," Baxter finished. "You keep reminding me of this fact. But let me remind you that without my yachts, without their willing crews that I spent years vetting, you would be in the same place you were when you came to me, stuck."

Perlstein huffed in frustration.

Before he could speak, Baxter said, his tone soothing now, "This is a minor setback, Efraim. I only wished to bring it to your attention so that you might give me your insight into how I should proceed."

It was an olive branch, one Perlstein wasted no time in snatching.

"Have you alerted the rest of the captains?"

"It is being done as we speak."

Perlstein nodded. "Then maybe it is time for *you* to speak with our friend Dr. Nahas. Perhaps he has some insight into what has transpired."

"And you would be content to listen to the conversation but not actively participate?"

Another olive branch. Baxter had a drawer full.

"Yes, I would be fine with that."

"Good, now why don't we join Ms. Krygier? I've been saving a very expensive bottle of aged whiskey just for you. After that we can hear what Dr. Nahas has to say."

"Agreed."

Baxter smiled and patted his co-conspirator on the shoulder.

"Oh, and one more thing, Efraim. Could you make a discreet inquiry with your intelligence contacts?"

"For what purpose?"

"Call me paranoid, but I still want to make sure the Americans have not become privy to our tangled web."

"I checked just before leaving, but yes, I can check again."

"Good. It would make me feel so happy if we could amaze President Zimmer with a splendid surprise gift. Don't you agree?"

The two man shared a smile and left the room. For better or worse, they were now connected. Baxter just hoped that Perlstein and the Israelis would hold up their end of the bargain. The world would soon find out what they had concocted, and Baxter did not want to be the only one caught in the crosshairs.

T he man in the gray wool suit stuffed the cell phone in his pocket and closed his eyes. It was just starting to mist, but he didn't care. He lifted his face to the sky as he allowed himself a moment of quiet.

Finally, some good news. Jeanette Locke was safely in the Bahamas. It was the first piece of positive news he'd had in over a week. It was his job to track Chance Baxter. He'd been handpicked for the mission earlier in the year and given the field agents, four of whom were now dead, including their most important mole, Captain Weir.

He'd known Weir, had even liked him. Some people said that getting close with your sources was a no-no, but it was often inevitable. Two patriots conversing over beers, talking about the old days in the British Navy when all you had to worry about was the next cruise or the next port.

The man exhaled. Weir was gone now. He didn't know the details, hadn't heard a thing from Weir in the end, but he did know that *Suprema* was sitting on sand covered in tons and tons of sea water. If only they could get a team down there.

The Mexicans authorities promised to do what they could, but their resources were limited.

"Damn," he cursed aloud, opening his eyes to take in the day. It was dreary. The same weather they'd had for days, centuries really. He wondered why he stayed in London. Yes, it was home, but the world was full of sunny places. He'd seen many of them during his time spent in the service, and he was already planning to ask for reassignment.

The rain didn't help his mood, and his thoughts drifted back to what had occurred in the preceding days. A leak. Four men gone. Did Baxter know? Surely he did. If he did know, who told him?

Everyday citizens thought the intelligence apparatus was crafted to be flawless. In reality, it was anything but. When you inserted people into the equation, and worse, added their ambitions and prejudices to the jumbled morass, who knew what the machine would spit out?

He'd personally seen the same intelligence dissected three or four different ways, the output miles apart in their assumptions. Some said the solution was to rely more heavily on technology, and to allow the drones and the wire taps to gather the intelligence. It was all nonsense, really. Without the operators and analysts behind the scenes, how would the oceans of information be processed? Yes, technology did help, but getting eyes on the objective with an 80% picture of the situation was much better than watching through a television screen 2,000 miles away.

People - they were both the problem and the solution. The issue for the man sitting on the cracked park bench was that people, not machines, had upended his investigation. He'd never lost a source before and now, in a matter of hours, he'd lost four.

It was not his sense of pride or his ambition that was taking the sting but his sense of duty. He'd failed in some capacity. He had to believe that. And yet, there were other forces in play. Someone had alerted the Baxter organization to the surveillance.

If he'd been in on the operation from Day One, from the moment they'd sniffed out Baxter's dealings, he might have a clue. But like a crime scene that had been tainted by too many passers-by, the trail of culprits was now virtually indistinguishable.

Because of the layers of bureaucracy, he had to report certain things to his boss and his boss had to report them to his. Red tape. Checks and balances.

It was a perfect way to lose a secret. The moment more than one person knew it, the chance of that secret's survival was slashed in half. Add more people in the chain and soon it was no longer a secret.

The man in gray wished for the old days, when handlers could keep things from parliament, and they were able to treat their sources like confidential informants used by reporters.

He exhaled again. There was no use crying about it now. He had to find a way to salvage the operation. The Locke girl hadn't turned up a thing and knew much less than Weir had reported. She'd stay under MI6's protection for the time.

He needed help and he needed it fast. The only problem was where to get it. His own headquarters had been tapped by the enemy. He couldn't go there. For a long moment he thought about going into the field himself. That idea fluttered away with the breeze. He was not a field agent.

Then a name dinged in his head. An old acquaintance. A friend across the pond.

In that moment he made up his mind. If his own family couldn't help maybe the Americans could.

TEL AVIV, ISRAEL

At almost the same moment, a similar discussion was being conducted in a warehouse, far from prying eyes.

"What about the prime minister? Do you think he is involved?"

The man smoking by the window snorted.

"How could he not be? His sister just left the country with our prime suspect."

His colleague shook his shaggy head.

"Then we're stuck."

"I did not say that."

"I hate it when you're like this. If you have a plan, tell me."

The cigarette dropped to the floor, its last embers scattering in the dust. The man stamped it out and stepped closer to his co-worker.

"We knew from the beginning that our organization might be involved. We took the proper precautions."

"But Osman is dead."

The man nodded gravely and pulled another cigarette from the pack.

"And that was unfortunate. He was a grumpy old soldier but a good man."

"Without Osman we have nothing."

"There's always Krygier."

"She could be halfway around the world by now."

The taller man lit his cigarette and shrugged.

"It doesn't matter."

"What do you mean it doesn't matter? Stop speaking in riddles. Tell me, what do we do?"

After a long drag, and an even longer plume of smoke, the other man said, "We cannot go to our usual friends. We cannot go to the government."

"What are you saying, that we just give up? We've been working on this for two years! I won't just..."

His colleague raised a hand. "I did not say we should give up. I am saying our resources are limited. Now, because it is clear that one country might be most affected by this plot, do you not think said country might like to know about it?"

"You think we should tell the Americans?" the seated man asked incredulously. "You saw what their president said. If word gets out..."

"That part is inevitable. Perlstein will see to that. He and his henchmen will twist this in the worst way possible for us. I'm sick of the lies. It is time someone unravels the truth."

His friend huffed in frustration. It was not like them to dump a problem on another team, let alone a rival country. But maybe his long-time team leader was right. Maybe the Americans did need to know. Maybe Zimmer would find that not all of Israel was conspiring against their ally.

"Okay. We should do it."

"Do you have anybody in mind?" the taller man asked.

"Let me think on it, but yes, I believe I do. We've exchanged information before, and I am sure he will be happy to receive this."

"It is just like history that we should dump this on the Americans. How many times have we taken advantage of their intelligence efforts?"

Both men chuckled. It was an old joke that rang of truth.

His friend said, "Yes, but in this case, the answers would aid both Israel and America."

GREAT SALE CAY: 3:03PM

Another wrinkle, Baxter thought, and hung up the phone.

He did not like using the phone and he only did so on official business. So when the call came in from America, he'd been more than a little perturbed. But his contact had been clear. The CIA had received messages from the United Kingdom and from Israel, not an hour apart.

The messages were anonymous, and via different agents, but the collection filtered through a central source. His contact deep inside Langley was tasked with monitoring incoming and outgoing messages relating to the Baxter corporations and Efraim Perlstein, just to name two filters.

"It sounded like more than a heads-up," the man had said, "They want us to figure it out for them."

While that might have been comforting the previous day, Baxter was no stranger to investigations, even from the FBI and CIA, but now was not the time. British and Israeli intelligence had been on his scent for months. They'd gotten close on a few occasions, most recently with the moles placed by MI6, but nothing had ever come of it. It was a new world, a world where the absence of a smoking gun allowed men like Baxter to skirt the law as long as they were careful.

And he was careful, very careful.

But now the Americans knew. It was inevitable, of course, but the timing...

The Americans...

Baxter's thoughts went to his guests. Could their visit be merely coincidental?

THE WHITE HOUSE

August 29th, 3:21pm

Marge Haines swept into the Oval Office as fresh as if she'd just woken up from a day long nap. President Zimmer was amazed by her stamina and spirit. He had to remind himself that he shouldn't be amazed. Not only was Haines a powerful attorney but also she'd manned the helm at SSI after Travis's departure.

He, on the other hand, felt haggard. He'd spent the day listening to droning lists of what was wrong with American aid packages.

There were the schools in Afghanistan that didn't have any books because local bandits had stolen them in the middle of the night. Why? Who knew? In addition one school in particular hadn't had electricity or proper plumbing for months. The infrastructure wasn't there. The inspector who'd briefed the president was almost in tears as she recalled the students having to use the back wall of the school as a urinal.

Then there was the multi million-dollar hospital they'd built in Iraq. The institution had been shiny and new in the beginning, but the fatal flaw had been something a first-world country seldom had to think about. Now, there were barely any doctors to staff the facility, let alone trained nurses to do what needed to be done.

So, the small staff had left in search of real jobs in Baghdad. The hospital was said to have switched hands from one local faction to another every few months until finally they'd left it to the beggars and vagrants. More millions wasted.

President Zimmer had listened for hours, learned of the food that had never been delivered or the troops who had merely watched as fifteen-year-old conscripts learned how to put on uniforms and boots.

It was all so pointless. How could they fix it? Zimmer told himself it would take one step at a time and a boatload of patience.

"We have two minutes until the director calls," Marge said without looking at her notes.

Zimmer had found in the short time they'd been working together that Haines had the ability to glance at a schedule once and commit it to memory. It was almost funny to see how put together she was. He could see why Travis liked her, maybe even loved her.

"Everyone being nice to you?" Zimmer asked.

"As nice as they should be. I'm the new kid, remember?" She didn't seem worried, and he wasn't concerned either. She'd have the White House staff whipped into shape even faster than Travis. Zimmer found it very comforting to have her there now. Yet another gift from Travis.

His phone rang a minute and a half later and his secretary announced that the Director of the CIA was on the line. When he was patched through, the director cut right to the matter.

"Mr. President, we've just received word from not only British Intelligence, but also Israeli intelligence that a plot is underway to destabilize the region."

"And by region you mean —?"

"North America, specifically, sir."

While that wasn't news to Zimmer, he didn't say as much to the director. He and Haines had decided to keep things quiet about Hannah Krygier and the Israeli conspiracy, at least until Cal had something tangible.

What did concern the president was the timing of the news.

"You said both British and Israeli?"

"Yes, sir. I know what you're thinking and I'm certainly at a loss about the timing."

"Do you think they could be working together?" Zimmer asked.

"I'm not positive but I don't think so. They came in through agents in totally different divisions. I haven't talked to them personally but the information seems legitimate."

"And what was the information in addition to what you've already stated?"

"They mentioned two names, sir. A British billionaire named Chance Baxter and an Israeli named Perlstein."

"What do they have to do with us?"

"I'm not sure, Mr. President. I have my people working on it now."

Zimmer looked to Haines and frowned.

"Director, I've got Marge Haines, my new chief of staff with me. Marge, what do you think?"

Marge moved closer to the phone.

"Director, was there any indication that the Brits and Israelis wanted to coordinate efforts on this?"

It took a second for the answer to come, like the director was checking his notes.

"No, Ma'am. The two agents asked as much but were told it was just an FYI kind of thing."

"So they want us to do the dirty work," Zimmer said, to no one in particular.

"It looks that way, sir," the director answered, his mood matching Zimmer's.

"So what do we do? You said your people are working on it?"

"Yes, sir. I'm happy to stop by when I have more information to report."

"You know me, if it can be solved with a phone call, you don't need to waste your time coming here."

"Thank you, sir."

Zimmer ended the call and looked up at Marge.

"So?"

Marge stared at him for a moment, like she was thinking.

"Something's not right here. I don't like the timing. I wouldn't be surprised if this was a calculated ploy to somehow knock us off the trail."

Zimmer wasn't about to disagree. It seemed too easy that the calls had been mere coincidence. No, there had to be something deeper going on, something they couldn't yet see.

The president was about to say that to Marge when Bob Lundgren burst into the room. The press secretary didn't greet either of them but grabbed the television remote from the president's desk and turned on the TV.

It flickered to life a second later, and there was the face of the Israeli Prime Minister. He was standing behind a podium looking stern. Zimmer had met the prime minister on a few occasions and while he seemed a little withdrawn, Zimmer liked him and his platform for Israel's future.

"Bob, what's going on?"

Lundgren didn't look back, but said, "My Israeli counterpart just gave me a heads-up. He said you'd want to see this."

"Did he tell you...?"

"Shh," Lundgren said. The press secretary had never shushed him. That made Zimmer even more curious.

The prime minster nodded to someone off camera and began. He spoke in English for some reason. *Interesting*, thought Zimmer.

"Thank you for coming on such short notice. This will not take long. All of you heard President Zimmer's recent speech at the United Nations. You've replayed the footage ad nauseam and many of us have had conversations with the president. I, for one, was glad to see that President Zimmer is doing what I've called for since my election." His voice went cold. "But I fear things are not as they seem."

Zimmer gripped the desk and glanced at Marge. Her eyes were glued to the television.

"Just this morning, credible intelligence indicated that American agents are currently operating on Israeli soil. I have been informed that two agents have been apprehended and they are in the process of being debriefed. Normally, this conversation might have happened behind closed doors, but as President Zimmer so eloquently said, 'It is time to come out from the shadows. So I ask you now, President Zimmer, what are your spies doing in my country?'"

GREAT SALE CAY

The Bahamas

Chance Baxter stared at the oversized painting of his mother, father and himself as the blade scraped up and down the hand-sized whetstone. Every so often, he would dip two fingers into the glass of water on his desk and dab the water on the whetstone. Then he would continue the sharpening.

One thousand passes per blade. It was a ritual. It was his zen. The memories of his childhood floated in the air and he thought about his mother, his poor mother. So beautiful, yet so damaged.

He'd known from a young age that she was mentally unwell. His father called her crazy to her face. She would just smile and go back to whatever she had been doing.

The younger Baxter had at first defended his mother when he was old enough to realize what his father was doing. He'd never received physical punishment for his youthful outbursts, but his father had locked him in his room for hours and he'd endured the screams and cries from his mother.

She would never cry when he was there, but the moment he left, every ounce of emotion spilled out. It got to the point where he rarely left her side. He didn't want to see her in pain and for a while it worked.

They played and laughed, even though under her cheerful facade, the nine-year-old boy saw the sadness eating away at her. He brought her paintings and doodles from school, and he was pleased when she was delighted.

Mother and son were inseparable, and soon she kept him at home, became his teacher. There were nights he would wake to find her curled up next to him like a child.

Some people might see it as unhealthy, but there was never any inappropriate conduct.

As for his father, the elder Baxter made it no secret that he was whoring about. He traveled constantly and sometimes came home with a wench on his arm. He even went so far as to introduce them to his wife and son.

Chance's mother always greeted them politely but she always held onto her son's hand like a metal vise. Chance would say hello and then stare at his father as if to say, "*What are you doing?*"

He knew it was wrong and he saw the pain it caused, but for some reason and, maybe it was the basest of human needs, he wanted to be loved by his father. Some part of him thought that if his father loved him, that one day his father would love Chance's mom again. It was a childish notion but young Chance did everything he could to care for his mother and please his father.

The day of his thirteenth birthday everything changed. He and his mother were celebrating in the kitchen. Because she couldn't bake, she'd ordered an enormous birthday cake.

There were knights on horses and kings on thrones. Chance loved it so much that he didn't want to eat it.

Then one of the maids had entered the room. Chance had never felt before the cold fury that he did that night as it radiated off his mother. She glared at the servant and said, "Get out."

The maid gave her a smug smile and left.

Their playtime was ruined after that. His mother sat on the floor and cried. He tried to console her with hugs and kisses but she was beyond his reach. Finally he asked her, "What is it, mother?"

She'd looked up at him with those sad eyes and said, "That was one of your father's whores."

He hadn't been shocked. Because he'd met them before, it didn't seem out of place. For some reason he didn't see it as his father's fault. Maybe his father was sick in another way like his mother was sick with sadness.

That night, as he lay in his bed, thinking about what he could do to help his family, he concocted a plan.

Even as a youth, Chance Baxter was patient. He waited a full week for the right time. When it came, he crept from his room, made his way to the kitchen where he extracted one of the many knives he'd seen the chefs use, and sneaked into the servant's wing.

He'd scoped out the room over the preceding week and knew exactly which one housed the culprit. The door wasn't locked. They never were. It was one of his father's rules.

He entered stealthily and stood inside, listening. The room was dark, but a sliver of moonlight sliced through the dark room, providing enough illumination to find his way.

There she was, snoring lightly, hair tied in a ponytail that cascaded onto her chest. She was beautiful in the moonlight and he stopped to admire her. She never moved and he did not hesitate.

The knife came down swiftly and slashed at her neck. Her eyes popped open and he slashed them too. She couldn't scream; blood was gushing from her mouth and throat. He kept slashing even through her writhing.

Then the squirming stopped and Chance stepped back to admire his handiwork. He felt no remorse, only relief.

Maybe now his parents could be happy. Maybe now his mother would be happy. Maybe now.

They'd found him the next morning sitting in the middle of the maid's room, still staring at the corpse. His father hadn't said a word as he lifted his son in his arms and carried him to his private bathroom. There, for the first time, he'd bathed his son.

He wasn't upset and he'd only asked one question.

"Why did you do it, son?"

The answer came without thinking. "For you and mother."

His father had nodded and finished the bath. After that day everything changed. Chance's education became his father's new undertaking. He hired a tutor who traveled with them everywhere and also served as a guardian. But for the majority of the time, when he wasn't learning about history or science, he was with his father.

Chance was sad to leave his mother's side, but the distance seemed to calm her. He was happy for that, but he was even more happy spending time with his father. Up until that point in time, he hadn't really known what his father did for a living. He knew they had money. You had to have money to live in a mansion and hire servants, but like most children his age, he didn't really understand where the money came from. His father showed him.

They visited the docks and chatted with shipwrights. They traveled to Hong Kong and shored up a long-term deal with exporters from China. Through it all, his father was patient and even doting. There were no hugs, but he did get the occasional pat on the head or firm handshake. It was all Chance needed and more than he'd hoped for.

There was another side of his father's world that he was introduced to soon after starting his apprenticeship. The first time it was a man who'd allegedly swindled some money from one of his father's ventures. The man was scared when he was brought into the elder Baxter's office in chains. He begged for forgiveness and his father granted it. The man was so overcome with joy that he never saw the blade behind his employer's back. It plunged into his temple and stuck there. A long moment later, the man fell sideways, his feet twitching as Chance watched, fascinated.

We are the same, Chance thought. My father and I are cut from the same cloth.

After that, his father had instructed him on the proper way to dispose of bodies. He taught it in a way that a physics teacher might teach a student about gravity. You do this, not that. If you don't want to get caught, you never do this.

And so it went. The years passed and Chance saw less and less of his mother.

One day there was a telegram. His mother was dead. For some reason he didn't cry. Deep in his soul, he knew it was for the best. Her pain was at an end. She could no longer be harmed.

He'd said a silent goodbye, and then he returned to the task of torturing a man who'd supposedly conspired to steal from his father. It turned out to be false, but one of the lessons Chance had learned from his father was that once you started you could not stop. It wasn't like he could let the man go. That would be absurd.

Chance was happy. He enjoyed his time on the sea and in the air. He grew up long before his time, but he was grateful for that. Anyone less mature would've crumbled at the loss of his mother. He had not and, to Chance, that win had been another attempt to please his father.

Now, father and son did not always see eye-to-eye. On business matters, son always listened to his father. But, when it came to women, their differences were insurmountable.

It produced a sort of asexuality in Chance. He admired the beauty of women and had never been attracted to men but something about the relationship between his mother and father, and more importantly, between his father and his whores, left a deep impression on Chance. It was one of the ways he saw himself as being superior to his father, and with the passing of time, his interest in the opposite sex waned.

He considered himself a sort of eunuch now. He'd read up on the ancient practice of castrating men. They were said to be both better fighters and protectors. In Chance's case, it made him a better businessman, a calming influence when the world was in upheaval around him.

Yes, it had been a good upbringing. His only regret was that he hadn't spent more time with his father toward the end. A massive heart attack had taken him in the dead of the night. Chance had personally taken care of the whore who'd come running with the news. They'd been together when it happened. Chance couldn't have witnesses so he'd attended to it, like he always had.

His mind clicked over to the thousandth pass, and Chance Baxter wiped the razor edge with a soft towel. Then he placed it in with the rest of his tools in a leather wrap with inserts for each. He patted them each one time, and he then rolled up the bundle and tied it tight.

Once his tools were tucked securely in his wall safe, he pressed the intercom on his desk. "George, will you please tell Mr. Layton that I am ready to see him?"

"Yes, Mr. Baxter," came the immediate reply.

"Oh, and, George, would you ask them to bring the puppy? I do love German Shorthairs."

"Yes, Mr. Baxter."

"Thank you, George."

He let go of the intercom button and sat back in his chair. The storm was coming, and like his father had taught him, it would soon be time to batten down the hatches.

THE WHITE HOUSE

August, 29th, 5:22pm

The briefing concluded seven minutes after it began, yet they were still no closer to an answer. The Israelis had fired the warning shot. However, the Director of the CIA didn't have a shred of evidence to corroborate this accusation.

"I'll say again, Mr. President, all agents in that region are accounted for."

"And you have no idea why they did this?" Zimmer asked, getting a nod of agreement from Marge Haines.

"I've reached out to my Israeli counterpart, but they're clamming up. It looks like they're taking this very seriously."

Zimmer nodded. His calls had gone unanswered as well. What would cause the Israeli Prime Minister to lie? He was one of America's staunchest allies, a man tied to the United States in so many ways. Maybe they did have two spies in custody and assumed they were Americans. He'd asked the CIA director as much and the answer was simple - anything was possible.

"Okay, let me know if you find out anything else."

"Yes, Mr. President," the director said, rising to leave. "Sir, I apologize and I know this might not be the best time but I wanted to bring one of the CIA's longest tenured employees by." He gestured to a bookish man with a wisp of slicked hair on his head who hadn't said a word for the duration of the meeting. "Mr. President, this is Rudolf Collier. Rudy's been with the Agency for thirty-five years. Today's his last day."

Zimmer rose and offered his hand. Collier gave the president a nervous smile and a limp handshake.

It's a pleasure to meet you, Mr. Collier. What is it you did for the Agency?"

The man cleared his throat and said, "I've been a presidential briefer for most of my career, sir. We've met before and I served you in that capacity. It was just after you assumed office."

Zimmer didn't recognize the man but he said, "I thought you looked familiar. Thank you for your dedication and service, Mr. Collier. I'm sure you've seen it all."

Collier nodded, but it was his boss who said, "Rudy knows where all the skeletons are hidden. He will be missed." He smiled at Collier and headed for the door. Collier didn't move.

"Mr. President, I just wanted to thank you for everything you've done. Good luck, sir." He offered his hand again and Zimmer took it.

After that exchange, the two CIA men left, the door closing quietly behind them.

"That was interesting," Marge said. "Did you really recognize him?"

Zimmer shook his head and chuckled. "I have a hard time remembering where I am half the time. Seemed like a nice enough guy, though. Thirty-five years is a long time.

* * *

THE CIA DIRECTOR EXCUSED HIMSELF, AND RUDY COLLIER

took in the long White House hall for the last time. He'd been there on many visits. He'd briefed six presidents. He'd seen and heard things that would make most Americans run for Antarctica.

He was a quiet, unassuming man. Soon after his arrival at Langley, he found those character attributes to be assets. He'd never wanted to be an analyst or, God forbid, a field agent. He loved books and his quiet nook in Georgetown.

Work was his second home and the archives his personal library. No one said a word as he came and went because he belonged there. Most people didn't know his name and that was fine with him. He liked to be unseen, unheard and inscrutable. He'd had enough scrutiny as a balding teen in high school. It was his job to organize and make sense out of the information. It might have seemed menial to some but to Collier no day went by that he didn't find some morsel to chew through with slow relish.

As he neared the exit, his heart slowed. That last moment with the president had been one of the most intense of his life. He'd looked Zimmer in the eye and said what he'd rehearsed. Rudy Collier wasn't a political man and he didn't care about which way others leaned. No, his was a quest for knowledge, secret knowledge to be specific. Conspiracy theories were his own personal nirvana, and he sucked those stories up like most Americans yearned for reality TV. He mined the troves of information in the vast CIA database to determine which historic events were documented truthfully, as well as those falsified.

It hadn't taken him long to secure his niche within the agency. No one wanted his job. It basically entailed presenting hidden information to an incoming president, then preparing for the next handover, often eight years away. It was monotonous and boring but Collier loved it. He might have stayed on another ten years; he could have. They would have let him, again, because no one wanted the job. It would probably fall on someone as a side duty, another in a list of endless tasks for some poor soul.

For Collier, it was time to leave. He had the last chip in his hand, well, in his head. He'd used four already. That information had netted him a tidy sum. Benefits of being with the agency included learning how to funnel money discreetly, making contact with operatives worldwide, and accessing operations and debriefings.

So, he'd only taken the five items he believed to be those hidden gems that could do little damage to the United States. After all, he wasn't a traitor, just an underpaid government employee looking to live out his retirement years in relative comfort. He didn't want to travel or buy expensive things. His dream was to move away from the bustle of Washington and find a small tract in the middle of the country. He'd never been married, thus relocation would be easy.

As a child he'd always dreamed of a library with every book he would ever need. Now he could build it, and would consume that knowledge like the legends of literature and philosophy had centuries before, in quiet solitude. He would build his tiny oasis and thrive there until his final days. That, to him, was heaven.

So, as Rudy Collier left the White House for the last time and climbed into his dented 2001 Honda Civic, the final chip bounced around in his head like a winning Powerball ticket.

One name. So simple and yet so gratifyingly rich. He wasn't the traitor; she was. They'd all been traitors to their home countries. The only difference was that Collier had just helped them meet their inevitable fates sooner than they'd planned.

Collier made up a tune as he hummed his way out the heavily-manned gate and into the dense D.C. traffic.

"Hannah Krygier, Hannah Krygier, oh oh oh, Hannah Krygier,"

he sang out of tune, over and over. It was his retirement song, a promise for the future. That faceless name, the name of a traitor, would soon be in the hands of someone who would snuff out the threat. Collier didn't care how or why. He just cared about the millions he'd been promised, half of which now sat in a bank account in Holland.

Collier smiled as he let a taxi cut in front of him, his mind drifting to dreams of days he would spend reading and absorbing the wisdom of the ages.

"Hannah Krygier, Hannah Krygier, oh oh oh, Hannah Krygier."

GREAT SALE CAY

The Bahamas

T he wind outside the reinforced windows howled. The occasional branch or piece of debris pummeled against the second-story window. Liberty whined at Cal's side, and he did his best to soothe her with long, calming strokes down her back. She shivered intermittently and stayed glued to his leg while Cal talked with the others.

Their meeting with Baxter had gone well. He'd walked them through his current inventory of yachts and he presented a host of others that could be purchased, if the right price were offered. If that happened, Baxter said he would be happy to broker the deal to ensure Jonas got the best deal he could for his money.

While Jonas took the lead on the money end, Neil quizzed Baxter on the technology and communications side. The billionaire answered without hesitation, a clear indication that he knew the working of sea-going vessels from top to bottom.

Master Sergeant Trent's depth of knowledge had surprised

Cal. His knowledge of the yachts was ten times what Cal's was. He'd asked Baxter about things Cal never would have put together. It was a good thing he was serving in an advisory role on the business end of things. Boats and ships weren't his thing. That was one of the many reasons he'd become a Marine and not a sailor.

"I don't know guys. I may just have to buy one," Jonas was saying.

Trent chuckled and elbowed Gaucho. "I told you."

Gaucho rolled his eyes. He hated being on the ocean more than the rest of them.

"Jonas, if you buy a yacht, I won't step foot on the damn thing. I swear."

The rest of them laughed, even Maya, who'd spent most of the meeting with Baxter listening like Cal. Her cover was that she was a security consultant. It wasn't a giant leap given what she'd formerly done for a living. After the meeting, they all relaxed. All indications were that Baxter was a brilliant businessman and a superb shipbuilder. Maybe TJG would find itself with a yacht at the end of the trip. If what Baxter said was true, just renting the thing out could be a sound investment for Layton.

"Neil, any luck with comms?" Cal asked. The storm was causing interference with their electronic and communication gear. When they'd asked Baxter about it, he'd confirmed that his internet service and satellites communications were down.

"Not yet," Neil answered, more frustrated than the others. He handled the lack of internet access as well as a fetus without an umbilical cord.

"So, no word from Brandon," Cal mused. It had been close to four hours since their last communication with anyone outside of Great Sale Cay. They knew the rest of the TJG team was in Freeport awaiting further orders. Fortunately, it didn't look like they'd be needed because the hurricane was closing in fast now. Taking anything out on the water was asking for trouble.

"No word from anyone," Neil said. "When do you think we can go home?"

Cal shook his head. "I think it's best if we hunker down here. Hopefully the CIA has a line on what's going on. This was all just a hunch anyway."

No one disagreed with him and the only one who jumped when the lightning flashed outside was Liberty. Then the lights flickered for perhaps the half-dozenth time in the last two hours.

Thunder boomed and Liberty yelped. This time she did jump right out of Cal's hands and she bolted for the open door.

"Crap," Cal said, and ran off after her.

"I'll come with you," Maya said, and ran after them.

* * *

EFRAIM PERLSTEIN'S GRIN DID NOT DIMINISH AFTER HE hung up the phone. Everything was falling into place. His cohorts in Israel were doing as he'd instructed. The prime minister had been led to believe that the Americans were conspiring against the Israelis. Yes, information was such a powerful tool. How he loved to manipulate information to get others to do his bidding.

He'd twisted the truth to turn other prime ministers where he'd needed, but now it was even better. Now the prime minister was playing defense for Perlstein's plot, and the Americans were once again on their heels.

Perlstein cackled as he handed the phone back to Baxter.

"I take it that everything went well?" Baxter asked. He was holding the only means of communication with the outside world. He'd told Layton and his men the truth. The hurricane was making it difficult to get any work done. It was a good thing he'd told his captains to hold in place.

"He went on television and told the world that the Americans sent spies into Israel."

Baxter nodded but did not join in Perlstein's glee. Manipulating politicians was just another day in Baxter's busy life. He was about to make his own phone call, one that would give them the answer that had started with Zimmer's proclamation at the United Nations.

He dialed the number from memory and waited. The man on the other end answered on the fourth ring.

"Yes?"

"Do you have the name?"

"I do."

"What is it?"

The man told him.

"Thank you. The money will be transferred within moments," Baxter said. He did not bother saying goodbye. Instead, he hung up the phone and stared at it for a long moment.

"Did you get it?" Perlstein asked, excitedly. The information was expected to help the Israeli more than his co-conspirator. It was intended to be an added bonus from a CIA contact who had assisted Baxter in the past. Rudolf Collier had always been accurate with his intelligence and that could not always be said for government employees. And as a result Baxter was only too happy to reward the CIA man accordingly.

But now the information was not what he'd expected. He wasn't supposed to know the name. Finally, he looked up at Perlstein, his face unreadable to the Israeli.

"What is it? What is wrong?" Perlstein asked.

Baxter glared at him.

"He provided me the name, the name of the traitor who you so longed to find. Oh, yes, he gave it to me."

"Well, who is it? What is the man's name?"

"It is not a man, you fool; it is a woman," Baxter growled.

Perlstein's face twisted in confusion. "A woman? Who is she?"

Baxter walked over to Perlstein, grabbed him by the shirt and said, "The mole's name is Krygier, Hannah Krygier."

* * *

CAL COULD JUST SEE THE PUPPY'S REAR END AS SHE rounded a corner and descended the stairs. He and Maya bolted past a surprised pair of maids as they tried to catch the pup. At each turn they just missed her as her four legs churned. Liberty whined the entire way. It was only the whining that helped them find her. At times, they stood at crossroads and listened.

She was going down, deeper into the complex than Cal and his friends had been. He estimated that they'd gone down four flights; in the back of his mind he wondered how far down they could go. The walls seemed thicker now and the decor became less lavish and more utilitarian. He barely noticed it as he saw Liberty skid at the end of the hall and half slammed into the wall. She regained her footing and bolted to her right.

"She's fast," Maya said. There was a girlish excitement in her voice, like they were chasing fireflies in the night.

Cal chuckled, sprinted around the corner, and exhaled when he saw that it was a dead end. There were two doors at the end of the hall, and Liberty was scratching on one of them.

They made it to the doors and Cal scooped the frightened puppy up in his arms.

"It's okay, Liberty. It's okay," he soothed. She nuzzled his neck and whined softly. At least they couldn't hear the thunder from where they were.

A moment later, the door Liberty had been scratching on cracked open. Cal was about to apologize when he saw the woman's face. She was older but still undeniably beautiful.

"I'm sorry, Ma'am, my puppy just got scared from the storm."

The woman smiled and opened the door further.

"That is alright. May I?" she asked, motioning to take the dog.

Cal nodded and moved closer. When he did he heard Maya inhale sharply behind him. The woman in the doorway shifted her gaze. Her face went blank and then pale.

"Maya," the woman whispered, backing into the room.

"Aunt Hannah?" Maya asked.

Cal looked back and forth between them. The woman's face had become a mask of horror and surprise. She was closing the door now but Maya stepped forward and shoved her foot in the opening.

"Please, you must go," the woman said. Her voice was desperate.

Maya pressed closer. "I don't understand. What...?"

"Go, Maya. Get off this island if you can. It is not safe."

"Why? Tell me why? I did everything that you said. Tell me why you are here."

Maya was halfway into the room when the woman sobbed, "Please, Maya, go."

Maya stood there for a moment not saying a word. And then she nodded like some silent message had been passed between the two women. She turned and stepped out of the doorway.

"We have to go," Maya said flatly.

Cal looked to the woman in the doorway and then to

Maya, who was already making her way down the hall. What had just happened? And then the name tumbled into place.

"Hannah Krygier?" he asked.

The woman's complexion changed from white to a dusky gray. Then she grabbed the doorknob, shut the door, and left Cal wondering how the hell they were going to get off the island and, more importantly, how they were going to get word to the president.

"There has to be a way to contact them," Zimmer said.

"They've tried everything," Marge answered, her phone to her ear. They were stuck. The weather in the Bahamas was getting incrementally worse, and now they knew that Chance Baxter was involved in the plot Perlstein and his Israeli counterparts had concocted.

Not knowing who to trust or ask for assistance only added to the feeling of grave unease. Quite literally, they were stuck. The Israelis weren't answering and if Baxter was involved, there was a very real chance that he'd infiltrated portions of the British intelligence establishment and quite possibly the government itself.

"We've got the rest of Cal's team in Freeport," Marge said.

"Are we in contact with them?"

Marge nodded.

"Call them and find out the conditions down there. See if there's anything they can do to reach Cal."

FREEPORT, BAHAMAS

"Yes, Ma'am. We'll do our best." Jim Powers hung up the secure line and looked up at his brother. "Things are bad, little brother."

"How bad?" asked Johnny.

"The guy who owns the island might be the one behind everything."

"Oh, shit."

"Yeah."

The brothers stood there for a moment. As the senior men on station, they'd been put in command of the TJG operators who were just waiting for Cal's call. It had been a precaution to bring them along, but thank God they had.

"Let's go talk to the boys and see what they think," Jim said, the former Marine already marching off to find the team leader.

TEN MINUTES LATER, THEY WERE STILL STRANDED. THE SEAS would swallow up anything they launched and their jet wouldn't help because jumping from any altitude was suicide.

Jim Powers reluctantly made the call to Marge Haines, who took the news stoically and told him the president would authorize any help they might need. Jim thanked her and hung up the phone.

As he did, Benny Fletcher, the former Army chief warrant officer and TJG's third pilot walked into the room.

"I think I've got something," he said, joining the Powers brothers at the table.

"What's up?" Johnny asked. The brothers liked Benny. He was unassuming on the outside, but he was a bad-ass pilot. You had to be if you spent your whole career flying out of Ft. Campbell. Those Night Stalkers were the best of the elite.

"I bumped into a couple Pave Low pilots in the airport lounge. They said they'd been grounded on their way back to Hurlburt. I was thinking we could commandeer one of their birds."

"Wait, are you saying you want to fly in that stuff?" Johnny pointed out the window where the palm trees were almost bent in half.

"I did some cross-training with the Coast Guard a few years back; I did some hurricane ops. I think we can make it over."

"Did you mention this to the pilots?" Jim asked.

"I thought I'd run it by you guys first."

They were quiet for a long moment, only the sound of the wind whipping across the island. Even if they could get the Pave Low, it was a huge gamble. With the capability to carry approximately 38 troops and a rugged time-tested system, the Pave Low could be perfect. But then there was the obvious downside. They'd be putting everyone's lives at risk.

"Benny, why don't you go ask the boys what they think. We'll see who volunteers and then I'll make the call to the president."

Benny left the room and was back two minutes later.

"They're all in," he said with a grin.

Jim shook his head. "I hope they know what they're getting into."

"We do," Benny answered, the grin stretching wider.

TWENTY MINUTES LATER, THEY'D SOMEHOW MADE IT across the tarmac to the airport. They burst in the door and received dirty looks from half the room. Benny picked out the group of pilots and headed their way.

"What's up, Fletch?" one of the pilots said. He didn't

bother to get up from where the four pilots were playing cards on the ground.

"We need your bird," Benny said.

Every pair of eyes looked up with amusement.

"You're kidding right?"

Benny shook his head. "I have someone on the phone for you."

He handed the confused pilot the secure phone which was thankfully still working.

There were a couple respectful "Yes, Ma'am" and "OK" before the pilot returned the phone to Benny, his face stamped with awe and wonder.

Benny gave the phone back to Jim Powers and said, "Can you take us out there?"

The pilot shook his head, like he was waking up from a dream. "Man, you are one crazy son-of-a-bitch, but if you want her, you've got her."

Ten minutes later, after a quick run-through, and after they'd given the MH-53 Pave Low's crew a chance to snag their gear, Benny shook the pilot's hand.

"Thanks again."

The pilot shrugged and said, "You break her, you buy her," and left to join his fellow pilots.

THE TJG OPERATORS WERE READY TO GO. EIGHTEEN TJG men boarded the Pave Low less than an hour later. They were accompanied by Benny, who would pilot the Pave Low, and the Powers brothers, who would serve as crew members.

Visibility was shit, and the night gloom didn't help.

After the harnesses were fastened and the systems were checked, what was left of The Jefferson Group lifted off into the edges of the hurricane. No one knew if they'd make it but they all knew they had to try.

THE WHITE HOUSE

Marge placed the phone in its cradle and let out a long exhale. She'd possibly just signed the death warrants of twenty-one men. Many she'd known at SSI prior to their move over to TJG. They were good men, warriors all, and firmly dedicated to Cal Stokes.

More importantly, they believed that this mission was critical to the safety of the United States of America. They were patriots who didn't think twice about going into harm's way, should the need arise. They'd done it countless times. They were the heroes that other veterans whispered about and wished they could be like.

The men of TJG never asked for applause; they never wanted the acclaim. It was one of many reasons Marge would miss her post at SSI. It was a unique opportunity to be among warriors who lived unselfishly and ran to the bugle call without a second thought.

Those thoughts weighed on her as she slumped on the couch and closed her eyes.

"So they're going?" the president asked, his voice soft with concern.

"They are."

"What do you think their chances are?"

Marge shook her head. She didn't want to repeat it aloud but she did.

"Jim Powers said he gave them a thirty percent shot of making it to Great Sale Cay."

"That's it?"

"That's what he said."

"Well, then I guess we should say a little prayer, don't you think?"

Marge wasn't the praying type, but she still found herself

begging God to watch over those brave men who she'd just sent to their possible deaths.

GREAT SALE CAY

The Bahamas

Hannah bit her tongue and kept her hands clutched to her stomach as she was escorted into Chance Baxter's office. Her mind was still reeling from seeing Maya. Maya! What was she doing on the island? Had Baxter somehow tracked her down through Perlstein? Perlstein knew about Maya, of course, but to Hannah's knowledge he'd never seen her. The snob was too concerned with being boss to worry about such frivolous details. Better to dispatch his underlings to kill Maya.

But Hannah had saved her from Perlstein's clutches. She'd shipped Maya off to America. Why was she here? Why?

Those thoughts rattled around in her head as she tried to look presentable and gather her wits. Baxter and Perlstein were drinking some dark liquid, probably aged whiskey. Perlstein's glass was almost empty while Baxter's looked untouched.

"Ah, Ms. Krygier," Baxter said, rising from his seat. "Thank you for joining us."

She searched his face for anything that might give her a clue of why Maya was here. His face gave nothing away. His face was as welcoming as it had been the first time she'd met him. Perlstein, on the other hand, glared at her from his chair while he drank deeply from his glass.

"We were just discussing our arrangement," Baxter said, pointing to the bar.

She nodded and he went to fetch her a drink.

"And what exactly were you discussing?" Hannah asked, trying to ignore Perlstein, whose face seemed to fall into a deeper glare.

"Your brother, the prime minister, does he know everything about you?" Baxter asked, plucking an olive from a small dish and placing it in her martini.

"What do you mean?"

"Does he know everything you do for a living?"

Was it just an innocent question or was he probing? Hannah couldn't tell with her senses already dulled from the shock of seeing Maya. She tried to put her emotions aside.

"I have helped him with his political career in the past. Is that what you mean?"

Baxter turned and presented her with a martini.

"I made it a little dirty. I hope you don't mind," he said.

Hannah sipped the drink and smiled appreciatively.

"It's perfect, thank you."

Baxter smiled and motioned to the sofa across from Perlstein, who was still staring at her but now with more distrust. What was his problem?

"So, as I was saying, how much does your brother know of your career outside of assistance you've provided personally?"

"I don't know really. We're not particularly close. Is that what you are asking?"

"I assumed but I wanted to be sure."

Where is he going with this questioning, and why is Perlstein trying to murder me with his gaze?

"And what about your extracurricular activities? Does he know about them?" Baxter asked, finally taking a slow sip from his own drink.

"I'm not sure I know what you mean, Mr. Baxter."

Baxter set his glass down on the coffee table and, for the first time since they'd met, the billionaire leveled her with steely eyes.

"Does he know you're a spy, Ms. Krygier? Does he know you've dedicated your life to providing information to the Americans while deceiving your own country?"

GEORGETOWN, WASHINGTON D.C

Rudy Collier felt like skipping. The CIA was having the rest of his personal items shipped to his new address, a quaint little farm he'd closed on an hour before. Iowa would be good for him. It was away from the bustle of big cities, far from the prying eyes of Washington. How he longed to stretch out in his leather recliner and immerse himself in his never-ending quest for the perfect book.

The night was warm but he could smell the coming rain. Someone at the office had said that the hurricane about to make landfall in the Caribbean would most likely dump inches of rain along the East Coast. He didn't care. Hopefully, he'd be gone in the morning. With the money that was now sitting in nine different accounts around the world, he could afford to have a moving company pack and ship his belongings without him having to lift a finger.

Yes, it would be nice to live with such luxuries. He'd lived frugally the day he'd left his parents' house at eighteen. He'd scrimped and saved, and now it was all paying off. A quiet life in the heartland beckoned and Collier couldn't wait for this new chapter to begin.

With his stomach full from what might possibly be his last Subway sandwich, he ascended the last rise that would lead him into his humble home. The agent he'd hired to put the house on the market said it would easily sell in a week's time. It had taken him every ounce of newfound entitlement not to negotiate her commission. It would be worth every penny if she did all the work. He smiled at that fact as he closed in on a couple coming from the opposite direction. The woman was laughing and her boyfriend or husband was tickling her.

Collier moved farther to the right to get out of their way. They barely seemed to notice him until the last moment. Then the man looked up in surprise as he veered in front of Collier, courtesy of a playful shove from the woman.

"Oh, man, I'm sorry," the guy said.

"No problem," Collier answered, ducking his head and walking past them.

The man caught him by the shoulder.

"Hey, can we buy you a drink? Peace offering?"

"Yeah, come on. We're celebrating and Ben's such a bore," the woman said, her words slurring.

"Uh, no thanks," Collier answered. That was when he noticed that half the lights on the block were out, including the two on his porch. *Strange.*

"Hey, are you Rudolf Collier?" the man asked.

Collier answered without thinking, his mind too engaged with the darkened street. "It's Rudy, and if you don't mind, I have to go."

"Ha, Rudolf. That's a funny name," the woman laughed.

But the man was close to him now, his grip tight on Collier's arm.

"Let go of..."

Collier's next words came out in a squeak as he felt something blunt and hard against his ribs.

"Mr. Baxter says thanks, Rudolf."

Collier's eyes bulged. The sixth name on the list. The name he'd made disappear before briefing Zimmer. The name he'd contacted and who'd made him rich. Why would Baxter...? Collier tried to scream as whatever the man had in his hand came up to face level. He realized it was a gun with a long silencer on the end just as the man squeezed the trigger.

Three wounds entered Rudy Collier's forehead in rapid succession. A second later, his body flopped, motionless, to the ground.

The gun was already back in the man's pocket as he turned and put his arm back around his partner's waist. She giggled again, kissed him on the lips, and the pair walked away as if nothing had happened.

GREAT SALE CAY

Hannah struggled to find the words. Perlstein seethed. Baxter waited.

"Why do you think I am a spy, Mr. Baxter?"

"Efraim, will you excuse us please?" Baxter asked. It wasn't a request but rather an order.

Perlstein said something under his breath, got up from his chair and, upon his departure, he grabbed a bottle of whiskey from the bar. Once the door was closed, Baxter continued.

"Do you think you were the only one?"

Hannah stomach turned. More riddles?

"What do you mean?"

"The Americans are very clever. They lost some of their nerve after 9/11 but they have since regained it."

"You've lost me, Mr. Baxter."

"I apologize, both for the intrigue, and for Efraim. He can be such a pest."

Hannah nodded, wanting to take a long pull from her drink, but not trusting her shaking hands. Baxter either didn't notice or didn't care.

Baxter went on. "Let me guess. You were recruited in university?" Hannah didn't move. "That was where they found me. Of course, the initial introduction was through my father who was always uncovering helpful ways to take advantage of foreign powers, but this time it was me they wanted."

"I don't understand what you are saying," Hannah said.

Baxter grinned. "Come now, Ms. Krygier. I'm telling you my secret, so why don't we dispense with the lie? It took me a lot of time and a good bit of money to find out the truth. Would you like to hear the story?"

Despite her own feelings, Hannah nodded.

After sipping his drink, Baxter said, "In the 1970's, someone in the American government had the brilliant idea of finding influential men and women in their early twenties to recruit for long-term missions. Much like sleeper cells they would, or should I say *we* would, lie dormant until we discovered some imminent danger that would affect the United States. The Americans ended up with six recruits, you and I being two of them. From what I've pieced together, the other four were from Japan, The Soviet Union, Mexico and Canada. A strange mix, I know, but clever in its own way. Well, the Soviet mole was discovered barely a year after being established. The KGB tried to ransom him back but the Americans flatly denied the man's existence as a spy. He was jailed and then found dead the next day. The Mexican spy died of natural causes. I found and killed both the Canadian and the Japanese moles."

He said it casually, as if he'd just explained his family recipe for bread pudding.

"So that leaves the two of us. As luck would have it, I had no idea you were the other mole until a recent phone call from a former colleague. At first I thought that killing you might be the best course. But once I had a moment to think and really digest the possibilities, I wondered if this might not be a blessing in disguise. So that brings us here, to this moment. Do you have any questions?"

Hannah's heart pounded in her chest. *Questions? How could he ask such a thing?* If Baxter wasn't some sort of sociopath, he was undoubtedly the best actor she'd ever come in contact with. She reminded herself that she had to keep her wits. That's what they'd said when they'd recruited her, a fresh-faced coed with the political contacts to establish an Israeli dynasty. There had been so much risk involved, but she'd viewed it as an exciting adventure. It also provided her the means to keep her country safe while forging a deeper bond with one of their most needed allies, the Americans.

"What do you propose?" she asked, trying to find that younger version of herself that hadn't been afraid of the monsters lurking in the dark of night.

"I'll have to think about it. With the storm coming..." The phone on his desk rang and Baxter looked up with the tiniest hint of annoyance. "Excuse me."

He got up from his seat and snatched up the receiver.

"Yes?"

Whatever the person on the other end said made Baxter frown. The acting was gone. Less than thirty seconds after the call had ended Baxter rejoined his guest.

"Is everything alright?" Hannah asked.

Baxter didn't answer her immediately. He was staring at the coffee table, his expression pensive. He looked up a full minute later and said, "I apologize, Ms. Krygier. Might I suggest we finish our conversation in the morning?"

He rose again and made his way to the door.

Hannah couldn't believe what she was hearing. Was he just going to let her go? And then she realized that there was no place *to* go. She was on an island in the middle of a hurricane surrounded by Baxter's servants who were most certainly spying for their master.

Baxter opened the door an inch and then stopped. He looked at her, his eyes calm, and he said, "Please stay in your room until George comes to fetch you in the morning, Ms. Krygier. It turns out that there are more American spies in our midst. I daresay they've taken advantage of my hospitality." He shook his head, his eyes bright once more. He smiled. "No matter. The nuisance will be dealt with before you awake. Good night, Ms. Krygier."

"Good night," she replied as she passed through the door. She thought only of Maya. Her presence and the phone call could not be a coincidence. She had to do something, but what?

GREAT SALE CAY

The Bahamas

AUGUST 29TH, 8:46PM

They'd moved to what Baxter said was a more secure location. The room was on the first level of the massive home and when you looked out the window all you could see was the steep drop-off to the ocean below. No beach, just water.

Master Sergeant Trent had been the first to test the window.

"Thick," he said as his knocking only elicited a deep thud. Amazingly, they couldn't even hear the storm raging outside.

They killed time by trying to come up with a plan. What they really needed was to contact their second team in Freeport or Zimmer in Washington. Someone needed to know that they'd found Hannah Krygier. They were sitting blind, deaf, and mute and no one was more frustrated than Neil. He worked furiously to try to get something to work. Nothing did, but he didn't stop.

Then the squawk came followed by another. Neil looked up. "Was that the radio?"

Gaucho walked over to the small encrypted radio they'd brought along as backup to all of Neil's fancy gadgetry. It squawked again, and this time a single word came out, "Inbound."

Neil jumped from his chair as everyone else gathered around. Even Maya, still shocked from the surprise of seeing Hannah, came over.

Neil fiddled with the knobs, trying to acquire a better signal. They were out of range of the main island, but if someone was coming to help…

This time the transmission came through clearly.

"Fletch inbound. I repeat, Fletch inbound."

"How the hell?" Neil asked.

Daniel grabbed the mike and keyed it, "Fletch, this is Snake Eyes. How do you copy?"

"Solid copy, over," Benny Fletcher said over the radio.

There was a collective sigh of relief in the room until Daniel asked in disbelief, "Are they flying through that?" He pointed to the window at the storm wreaking havoc across the island. Then he keyed the mike again. "What's your ETA, over?"

"Ten mikes," came the reply, this time sounding more garbled than before.

Cal stared at the radio, amazed that anyone could fly through the gale-force winds. Benny Fletcher was in a for a few free beers if he made it.

"Roger. Let us know when you're close. Snake Eyes, out."

Daniel set the mike back on the table and looked at Cal. "Looks like we just caught a break."

* * *

CHANCE BAXTER READ THE REPORT FROM HIS HEAD OF security. So, someone was stupid enough to brave the wind and torrential rains to reach his island. Baxter had to tip his hat to the brave fool, but that would have to wait.

"Make the necessary preparations please," Baxter ordered.

The security chief nodded and ran down the hall.

"What is going on?" an annoyed Perlstein inquired as he staggered out of his room. He still had a glass in his hand, and it was obvious by his lilt that he hadn't stopped drinking since leaving the meeting with Hannah Krygier.

"We have uninvited guests coming," Baxter answered.

That seemed to sober Perlstein up a bit.

"What? Who?"

"It seems as though some noble warrior is trying to rescue his friends."

"Who?"

"It is most likely Americans coming to the rescue of their friends."

Spittle came out of Perlstein's mouth when he spoke.

"Americans? Here?"

Baxter wanted to slap the man.

"It was inevitable, really. Don't worry, I have things well in hand."

"How? How could you deal with American soldiers?"

Baxter smiled patiently and said, "You don't think I'd build this house without a few surprises, would you?"

* * *

THERE HAD BEEN ONE MORE TRANSMISSION FROM Fletcher. The helo was five minutes out. Maybe luck was on their side. Cal hoped it would stay that way. He was about to say as much when a loud clicking sound hushed the room.

"What was that?" Trent asked. Then he pointed to the air vent on the ceiling. "That thing was open a second ago."

Then they heard the clicking sound again, and this time it

was followed by a loud scraping, like steel grating against steel. It stopped suddenly, but they all felt the final vibration in their feet.

Cal scanned the room. Nothing looked amiss except for the air vent. Then he tried the door. It was locked. He pulled on it, still nothing.

"Top, give me a hand," he said.

Trent came over and gripped the handle. He pulled and Cal could hear the door creak in complaint. Then, with a final yank, the door came off its hinges.

That wasn't the end of it though. There, behind where the door had just hung was another door. Cal knocked on it. Steel. He searched the seams but it looked airtight.

"What the hell?"

Then he heard a lighter scraping sound and turned to see four rectangular holes in the wall where a moment ago there had just been plaster.

"Get to the other side of the room," Cal said, every muscle in his body tensed for what was coming next.

He didn't have to wait long. He scooped Liberty up in his arms as the next surprise came. With the force of a fire hose, water sprayed from the holes in the wall, slamming Gaucho against the wall. Trent went to help him as the others stayed clear of the powerful streams.

The water hadn't been running for thirty seconds and already the water was up to their ankles. Everyone was looking around the room trying to find an escape route. Trent went at the windows with a chair, while Daniel stood on Gaucho's shoulders as he tried to pry one of the air vents open. It didn't take them long to figure out that they were trapped. By that time, the water had risen to their waists.

GREAT SALE CAY

The Bahamas

AUGUST 29TH, 8:52PM

The gusts had batted them around since takeoff. More than one of the TJG warriors in the back had availed himself of the conveniently placed barf bags. It was the worst conditions Benny Fletcher had ever flown in, and that was saying something based on his thousands of hours in the air.

"Island in sight," he announced to the Powers brothers. Johnny Powers was in the co-pilot's seat.

It took Johnny a second to find the island with his night vision.

"Got it," he said. "What are you aiming for?"

Benny laughed. "Whatever's biggest."

Another torrent of wind buffeted them left and the Pave Low lost altitude. Benny muscled it back, the veins in his neck bulging as he tried to get them back on course. When he did, he glanced over at Johnny who gave him a thumbs-up. There had been a lot of thumbs-up since they'd taken off from Freeport. Both pilots knew they'd need all the luck they could muster, and if a thumbs-up helped bolster their chances, then thumbs-up were free for the day.

Benny could make out the house now. There were spot-lights and most of the windows were illuminated. He decided to steer clear just in case another gust of wind blew them into the impressive structure.

And that's when he saw the flashes from the ground. The glass in front of his eyes splintered. Muscle memory kicked in and he banked right, away from the mansion and away from the gunfire. He couldn't hear it, but he could imagine that whoever was down there was probably putting holes all over the big bird.

"We've got one hit in the back," Jim Powers's voice said over the radio.

"All systems green," Johnny Powers announced.

At least there was that, and now they knew what they were getting into. There'd been the conversation before lift off when the TJG team leader asked the pilots if they knew what the threat might be. Johnny Powers had shrugged and said, "If it shoots at us, we shoot back."

With that question answered, Benny imagined the boys in the back were clutching their weapons tight. Now, if he could only get them on the ground.

* * *

BAXTER WATCHED AS THE PAVE LOW BANKED AWAY FROM the house, and he marveled as the tracers from his crack security team streaked into the sky. They were the best. Some were French Foreign Legion, and the others came from a combination of special forces and high-level police forces, similar to American SWAT teams. There were only ten men total, but they knew every inch of the island as well as the Baxter complex.

Baxter smiled and looked down at his desk. There was an old-fashioned meter that looked like a thermometer, except it had dark-blue liquid, and it was almost to the top. In another minute or two, he would press the button at the bottom of the meter.

He looked over at Perlstein who was trying to sober up with a cup of coffee.

"You look worried, Efraim. Is the coffee not helping?"

Perlstein scowled. "I thought you said they couldn't get to the island."

Baxter shrugged. "It wasn't a certainty but now that they're here, why not let my men have a little fun?"

Perlstein didn't reply. He was a politician, not a warrior. He didn't understand the thrill of the hunt. He'd never experienced the adrenaline rush of seeing a man die. It was what man was built for - war. Baxter's family had been fighting wars since his ancestors first stepped foot on the island of Great Britain. It was what they'd been bred for and it was how they raised their children.

Yes, it was good to purge the needs from his blood. Baxter just wished he could look into the eyes of the dying men before they plunged to their deaths.

* * *

THEY WERE ALL TREADING WATER NOW. CAL WAS TRYING his best to keep both his and Liberty's heads above water. The dog didn't struggle. That made things easier, but it still kept Cal's hands full. He couldn't let her go.

There was maybe a foot of air left between his head and the ceiling. They were all searching in vain for a way out. Luckily, no one was panicking. Even Maya was swimming back and forth, her strokes strong as she tried to pry another air vent open.

Then something changed. It took Cal a couple seconds to figure out what it was. The water. He no longer felt the rush of the spouts on his bare feet.

"The water's off," he said, the room was now eerily quiet except for the sound of lapping water.

"Is that it?" Neil asked, clutching onto the wooden sofa he'd been sitting on minutes before.

No one said a word as they listened. Nothing. Not a sound. Liberty whined for the first time since the water had entered the room. Then Cal heard a squeal, like a huge rusted door creaking open.

"Shit!" Gaucho cried out. He was the closest one to the window.

Cal's eyes widened when he saw what his friend had noticed. There was a crack at the top of the window, like it had somehow folded down. It remained that way for a moment with everyone staring at the only thing keeping them from plunging off the cliff and into the agitating water below.

Then, without warning, the entire windowed wall folded outward into the night sky, and Cal and his friends were flushed out of the flooded room into the hurricane-whipped sea.

* * *

IT SEEMED LIKE EVERY WARNING LIGHT IN THE COCKPIT was going off.

"We're losing her," Johnny said.

Benny was trying to bring the bird back around. The bastards on the ground had gotten off a couple of lucky shots, but that hadn't been the worst of it. The TJG warriors had gotten lucky when the island defenders decided to launch an anti-air missile their way. At that range, it should've been a direct hit. Benny knew that from painful experience. But the storm must have done something to the missile because they only got a glancing blow from the projectile. It managed to severely damage the Pave Low, but at least for the moment they were still in the air.

He couldn't see anything with the wind kicking up debris all over the ground. It looked like something out of a post-apocalyptic movie where a nuclear blast scorched everything in its path. Benny had to find a place to land, but where?

"Tail rotor's going down," Johnny said. Benny already felt it. The control felt heavy, like the steering fluid going out of a car. She wasn't responding to his gifted touch anymore.

Benny gritted his teeth then said, "I'm taking her in." Then he aimed for the only thing he could, the only beacon that any sane person would avoid at all costs. With a grunt and a mighty push on the controls, Benny took her down.

* * *

BAXTER FROWNED WHEN HE LOST SIGHT OF THE helicopter. He'd so been enjoying the scene unfold. It was a good thing he'd outfitted his men with anti-air capabilities. When his security chief had asked about them, Baxter had calmly explained that if he wanted the island to one day be a fortress they should start with the right weaponry to defend against an assault.

Now he wished they'd installed heavy machine guns on the roof, but that wouldn't be proper considering the clientele he brought to the island.

As he got closer to the twelve-inch thick glass, he got his answer. The building shuddered despite its fortress-like construction. The lights flickered.

"They crashed onto the roof," Baxter said, admiring the daring. Maybe it was time to leave.

"Efraim, grab your things."

"Where are we going?"

"Somewhere safe. Come, we'll get Dr. Nahas on our way."

"What about Hannah?"

Baxter thought about it for a moment. "Leave her. If she survives, we can always come back and fetch her."

They hurriedly departed the room and passed Baxter's armed men sprinting for the roof. Baxter wished them luck as they ran by. It wasn't that he cared; it was what he paid them for after all. But it was the polite thing to do.

GREAT SALE CAY

The Bahamas

AUGUST 29TH, 9:01PM

Cal's legs kicked furiously as he tried to stay vertical. It helped, but it couldn't stop him from face planting in the water, the jolt feeling more like a smack on concrete. He plunged deep, the water around him swirling angrily like he'd jumped into a pool full of gigantic eels.

Somehow he'd held onto Liberty but she felt lifeless in his arms. Cal didn't have time to think about that as he pushed for the surface with one arm while he kicked mightily with his legs. His face broke through the water's surface and, as he was taking a long breath of air, a wave slammed into him forcing water down his aching throat.

Up he bobbed again and this time his bearings were better. He had to stay away from the cliff lest he be crashed against the sheer wall. Liberty moved, then squirmed in his grasp. He held her tight as he sidestroked away from shore. His mind searched for a way to shore. He should have paid more attention when they'd flown in. Suddenly, he recalled the map they'd looked at in Charleston and he knew where to go.

He called out every few seconds as he swam, the stamina from miles and miles of ocean swims over the previous months keeping him going. Finally, he heard someone. He swam towards the voice and found Neil and Jonas clutching the wooden sofa.

"Are you okay?" Cal called over the screaming wind.

"I'm okay," Jonas said.

"Got a little banged up, but I'm okay," said Neil.

"We need to go that way," Cal yelled, pointing down the coastline.

The others nodded and began kicking that way.

Cal kept going, still calling out to his other missing friends. No one answered as they swam further, every inch a tortuous task as they were slammed time and time again by the raging sea.

* * *

HANNAH SAT ON THE EDGE OF HER BED, LISTENING. EVER since the conversation with Chance Baxter, she'd been locked in her room waiting for word. Would Baxter go back on his word and kill her? Where was Maya? How could she use Baxter's altered plan to her advantage?

Then the sounds came. First came the clicking and the scraping sounds like mechanical robots preparing for battle. She thought she'd heard water like a giant toilet being filled, but she couldn't be sure. Then the lights in the room had gone off and the emergency red light in the corner snapped on.

There was an alarm going off somewhere nearby. She could only hope it wasn't a fire. As deep as she was in the complex, she would be burned alive for sure.

So she waited and she listened, hoping for an answer.

* * *

THEY'D COME DOWN HARD. SO HARD THAT BENNY WAS surprised to see that they hadn't taken more of the building with the crash. The guys in the back had taken the brunt of the crash. Two suffered broken legs, one was unconscious, and one was dead.

Despite the casualties, the rest of the men were all business, already having secured the perimeter of the crash site.

Jim Powers came into the cockpit cradling an automatic weapon. He looked every bit the Marine he was. *Every Marine is a rifleman*, he remembered hearing once. Benny wished he were as comfortable around firearms as Jim. His gift was flying, not shooting.

"We're going in," Jim said.

"You too?"

"I'll let the pros take the lead, but I'll bring up the rear. You think you can hold things down here?"

"Yeah."

Jim nodded and went to join the others. That left Benny in the cockpit of a destroyed Pave Low, wondering what the hell he would do with his pitiful pistol should the defenders make their way up to the roof.

* * *

BENNY SHOULDN'T HAVE WORRIED. TJG OPERATORS, despite the heavy fall, were superbly trained and well armed. Plus, they held the high ground, something the defenders hadn't anticipated. So, when Baxter's men tried to ambush them at the first stairwell TJG men ripped through them. Their anger at being downed, the thought of their fallen comrades, and the hope that Cal and the others were still alive fueled the warriors.

They only stopped long enough to make sure the defenders were dead and to pick up a couple extra flash-bang grenades along the way. With their first obstacle obliterated, they moved quickly but carefully, clearing rooms as they went. Further into the complex they went room by room and floor by floor.

* * *

BAXTER ENTERED HIS TEN-DIGIT PIN AND THE PNEUMATIC door opened. Inside was a padded room with a simple array of technology on one corner. The room was fifteen by fifteen and included a row of four padded chairs on one side, each adorned with matching harnesses.

"What is this place?" Perlstein asked, staying in the doorway.

"It's my safe room, of sorts."

"Safe room? This thing won't keep them out!" Perlstein argued, pointing back the way they'd come. He was panicking now and Baxter was getting tired of it.

"Do you want to get away or don't you?" Baxter asked. Then his voice became calm. "Trust me, Efraim. Have I led you astray thus far?"

Perlstein glared at the billionaire but stepped into the room, followed by the less tentative Dr. Nahas. As soon as the two men entered, Baxter pressed a button and the door slid shut.

"Have a seat," Baxter said, pointing to the harnesses. "I have some preparations and then we'll be on our way."

"On our way?" Perlstein was trying to strap himself in.

"Oh yes, didn't I mention? This is an escape vessel as well.

We'll be safely off the island soon. Now buckle up. The fall isn't far but we don't want to hurt ourselves."

* * *

HANNAH TENSED WHEN SHE HEARD A KEY JANGLING ON THE other side of the door. A moment later the knob turned and through the red-lit gloom she saw the the face of George, the house manager.

"Please come this way," he said politely, apparently unfazed by all that was happening in his master's home.

Hannah hesitated. George beckoned with his hand.

"Please, there isn't much time, Ma'am."

Slowly, she stood and walked to the door.

"Is he going to kill me, George? Is that lunatic going to kill me?"

George smiled up at her, his white teeth gleaming.

"Not if I can help it, Ma'am."

And there it was again – hope. It was the only thing besides a gun to the head that could make her move from the relative security of the room. She followed George as they went down, not up. Shouldn't they be going to the surface, away from the house?

Hannah kept the question to herself as she followed the sure-footed servant deeper into the complex. He seemed to know exactly where he was going.

* * *

JIM AND JOHNNY POWERS FOLLOWED THE TJG TEAM AT A safe distance. It wasn't that they couldn't take care of themselves. They'd both shot their first .22 at the age of five, but they were not trained in urban combat like the men taking the lead. They watched in amazement as Cal's men tore through the house defenders. It shouldn't have surprised them, but the brothers had never seen the boys in action.

Down they went, further and further into the expansive complex. They felt it when they were below ground. It was colder and almost smelled like the bowels of a ship. From time to time they would surprise some of the household staff.

No one knew if Baxter's servants were in the know, so the operators zip-tied their hands to the nearest piece of heavy furniture and then moved on. It was the best they could do. They couldn't take prisoners with them. It would slow them down, and speed was imperative.

* * *

CAL'S BARE FEET TOUCHED CORAL AND HE KNEW THEY'D made it. He still couldn't see the shoreline, but he knew it was there. If the raging waves couldn't stop them, a short swim to land wasn't going to either.

A short time later they'd made it, but the near hurricane-force winds still made it almost impossible to stand. They moved from tree to tree, taking whatever cover they could. Flying palm branches slashed his face and Cal could barely see through the blinding and screeching winds.

But they kept going if for no other reason than to find shelter. Not knowing if his friends had survived drove Cal to continue moving against the tempest. That, along with the knowledge that something could yet be done to rid the world of Chance Baxter.

GREAT SALE CAY

The Bahamas

AUGUST 29TH, 9:10PM

They reached the front door which was thankfully unlocked. Cal put Liberty on the floor and she spun around in a happy circle before peeing on the floor. He'd have to work on that.

"You guys okay?" Cal asked.

Neil was breathing hard and leaning with one hand against the wall. "Still in one piece."

Jonas nodded but didn't say anything. He'd taken a nasty hit from a flying tree limb, and he had his shirt pressed against the left side of his face.

"Find a small room or closet. Stay there until I come to find you," Cal said. Even as they did, he heard footsteps coming from the winding staircase. He put his finger against his lips and motioned to the nearest room.

There they waited as the footsteps came closer. Cal stepped out of the room and waved.

A host of weapons were trained on him in a split second.

"Cal?" one of the TJG operators asked.

"Have you seen Top or Daniel?" Cal asked.

The man shook his head. "We came from the roof. Benny crashed our bird."

Cal didn't have any idea what the man was talking about. There would be plenty of time to find out later.

"Who has an extra weapon for me?"

Two men held up weapons for their boss. Cal walked over, grabbed one along with two sets of extra magazines, checked the chamber (although he knew it was loaded) and asked, "Where to?"

"We've cleared everything from here up. We're going down."

"What kind of resistance?"

"Heavy at first, but after the initial battle, we've only found house staff."

Cal nodded and pointed to the hallway. "Then lead on, dear friend. Lead on."

The man grinned and took point. Cal followed right behind. He wanted to be there when they found Baxter. For some reason, Cal found himself hoping that the bastard would put up a fight. Every muscle in Cal's body throbbed with anticipation. He had his friends' lives to avenge.

* * *

He had designed the safe room/escape pod to drop into the conveniently deep ocean hole below and then be pushed by the current out to sea where it would wait until the homing beacon brought in assistance. Baxter was just finishing the pre-plunge checklist when a warning appeared on the computer screen. Someone was trying to open the door. The warning only came up when the buttons of the keypad were pressed.

Baxter was the only one with the code so he wasn't

worried. He busied himself with the final preparations which included coding the encrypted homing signal. Thus, he was surprised when the computer screen flashed again. The door started sliding open.

"Oh, it's you," Baxter said, stepping to the door.

"I thought you might like to have her along, Mr. Baxter," George said, grabbing Hannah's arm and pulling her forward.

She would have kicked, punched, or done anything if she thought she had the slightest chance of getting away. But her supposed rescuer had just handed her back to the very man she'd wanted to run from. And that man, the billionaire with the charm of a harpy, now stood in front her, a long filet knife in his right hand.

"Just tell me what you did with Maya. Where is she?" Hannah asked, the desperation taking over.

"Maya?" Baxter looked confused.

Hope sprang once again in Hannah's chest, only to be crushed for the last time, this time with the words, "Ah, you mean the young lady." Baxter shook his had sadly. "I'm sorry to say she is no longer with us. Now, if you don't mind, we really must go."

Hannah's legs crumpled, but George caught her in his strong hands. He half dragged, half carried her over to one of the empty seats and strapped her in like a child. Then he went back to his employer and asked, "Is there anything else I can do for you, sir?"

Baxter patted the man on the shoulder fondly.

"No, George, thank you. Thank you for everything. Do buy us a minute or two, will you?"

"Yes, Mr. Baxter. Good luck."

He gave his familiar half bow and left the compartment. The door slid closed and Baxter said to the others, "That George is a wonderful man, maybe the best who's ever served the family. He will be missed." He let out a barely audible chuckle.

And with that, Baxter pushed a couple of buttons and the chains holding the pod in place began to creak overhead. Baxter strapped himself into the last remaining harness and he grinned at his unwilling occupants.

"I hope none of you get motion sick. It should be a fun ride." He rubbed his hands together expectantly and the pod commenced its slow descent.

* * *

THEY'D REACHED WHAT CAL BELIEVED WAS THE LOWEST level of the building. The place really was massive. The man running point was just peeking around a corner when a shot rang out up ahead. He ducked back.

Cal grabbed a flash-bang from the man's vest and chucked it down the hallway. In response, a flurry of rounds bit into the wall across from them. A split second after the flash-bang went off, they made their move. They'd practiced the next part so many times that it was second nature as they rushed around the corner, scanning for targets.

Cal saw him before his partner did and, as the pistol came up, Cal fired his own volley. The rounds tore into the prostrate form and the pistol clattered to the ground. They kept moving and they didn't let up until they'd confirmed George was dead.

"What was he doing down here?" the lead man asked.

Cal pointed at the door and stepped up to the keypad. It had been destroyed and he was certain it wasn't by his own rounds - probably by the dead house manager.

"Did you bring a breach kit?" Cal asked. The man nodded and went back to get it. When he returned, it took him less than a minute to mount it to the door.

They ran back around the corner and ducked down. The charge blew and the explosion rocked the hallway. After assessing the damage, they found it had bent the sliding door inward and it dangled off the edge. Cal looked over. The shaft was lit from below, and there was a chain running from a winch at the top of the shaft down to the water. There was something in the water, and it was glowing like a submerged chem light.

"What the...?" and then he realized what it was. "Who's got rope?" Cal asked. Someone produced a coil of black rope. "Tie the other end off." He handed his weapon to one of the men and stripped down to his boxer briefs. Before anyone could stop him, Cal took the other end and dove into the dark water below.

* * *

"THIS IS WHERE THINGS MIGHT GET INTERESTING," BAXTER announced. The descent had gone smoothly and now they were drifting on the natural current that would take them into the bay and then out to sea. He'd designed the craft himself. He knew every capability it had and the only feature he wished he had added was a form of propulsion. No matter, the ocean would do the work, and like a hamster ball inside another hamster ball, they would remain relatively level the entire ride. There was enough oxygen stored to last them three days and, the further they went out to sea, the craft was programmed to sink increasingly deeper. Once they'd signaled for help and help was on the way, it was as simple as releasing an inflatable tether that would float to the surface, get snatched by the rescue helicopter, and they would be airlifted to safety.

He'd gone simple with this one. Baxter's fear had been the more advanced the escape pod was the more likely it could be found. That wouldn't do. So, instead they would hide and wait. They would live like astronauts in space, suspended, a bit uncomfortable, but otherwise safe. Baxter closed his eyes and waited. *I should have brought a book*, he thought. *I'll have to remember that for the next time.*

* * *

CAL WAS ALMOST OUT OF BREATH WHEN HE FINALLY reached the craft's hull. He scrambled to find where it had been attached before, and he found it just as the blackness came to the edges of his vision. After breaking the surface and taking a few seconds to catch his breath, he swam back to the opening, now clearly marked by the flashlights of his men overhead. The current was strong, but at least he was sheltered by tons of rocks above from the onslaught of the storm.

There was another rope dangling near the surface when he made it back. He grabbed it and looked up, "Pull the other rope, but take it slow." The last thing they needed was for the rope to break.

It did not break and, even though it took longer than he thought it would, Cal watched as it inched back toward him. When it reached his position, he took the hefty chain and latched it back onto where it had been minutes before.

He gave the guys at the top of the shaft a thumbs-up, and then he and the craft were slowly hoisted into the air.

GREAT SALE CAY

The Bahamas

AUGUST 29TH, 9:37PM

The use of explosives was not an option because Cal didn't know who was inside the pod. Johnny Powers came up with the solution.

"How about we knock?"

There were incredulous looks all around but, after a minute, Cal did just that. He rapped on the sealed door with the butt of his rifle and waited.

* * *

THE FOUR PASSENGERS HADN'T FELT THE SHIFT. BAXTER'S design was so flawless that when Cal caught them during their outward drift, and they were once again hauled back into the complex, none of the occupants ever felt it.

So, when the tapping sounded at the door Baxter's first thought was that they'd somehow drifted into some underwater abyss and were being crushed by the immense pressure of the deep ocean. How long had he been asleep? And then he remembered that there was no such chasm near Great Sale Cay.

The tapping resumed and Baxter frowned.

Perlstein asked, "What is that?"

Baxter leveled him with a bored look and said, "Someone's obviously knocking on the door."

Baxter ignored the shocked look on the Israeli's face and unfastened his harness. As nonchalantly as if he'd planned it this way, he typed in the correct code, and the door slid open.

He was greeted by the muzzles of multiple automatic weapons.

"Good evening, gentlemen," Baxter said grandly. "I assume you'd like to chat."

* * *

"COME OUT, SLOWLY," CAL SAID, HIS SIGHTS TRAINED ON the billionaire and master of Great Sale Cay.

If the man was worried, he didn't show it. Once Baxter was safely cuffed by one of the TJG operators, Cal entered the escape pod. He recognized Dr. Nahas immediately. The man looked like he'd just seen a ghost. There was another man there and Cal was about to ask who he was when the man spoke up.

"I am an Israeli citizen, a friend to the prime minister himself, and I demand that you take me to the nearest consulate immediately."

You had to admire the man's bluster but Cal saw the fear in the man's eyes so he ignored him. He attended to Hannah Krygier instead, gently unbuckling the harness that held her in place. Her skin was cold and her eyes vacant.

"Where is Maya?" she asked, her voice just above a whisper.

"I don't know, Ma'am," Cal answered honestly. The last

time he'd seen Maya was just before they'd plunged off a cliff. She was probably dead. He didn't want to tell Krygier that, although he believed it to be true. He helped her up and he handed her off to one of the operators.

"Take Dr. Nahas with Ms. Krygier. Bring this one up to Baxter's office," Cal ordered. Then he padded back down the hallway, gun in hand, feet still bare, wearing nothing except his boxers.

WHEN CAL ENTERED BAXTER'S OFFICE, HE WAS WEARING the only set of clothing he could find. Liberty was once again at his side, and she didn't seem to mind all the TJG newcomers. She pranced along like she'd won the day and maybe in a way she had.

"Where is Layton? I want to talk to Layton," Baxter insisted as soon as he spied Cal entering the room.

"Why? So you can buy some goodwill from a fellow billionaire? Well, sorry pal, but I'm in charge here."

Baxter actually had the nerve to turn his nose up at him.

"You have no idea who you're dealing with, young man."

Six months prior, Cal might have done something different. He might have walked across the room and decked the smug asshole.

However, he'd been through the pits of hell since that time. He'd lost Travis and, if he was being honest with himself, he'd almost lost his own life. That fact hit him hard as he stared back at the billionaire. Men like Baxter were what was wrong with the world. They thought that their billions of dollars provided them a free pass to whichever show they chose. No, that wasn't right. Men like Jonas were the good guys, using their money to serve the greater good, not merely to inflate their egos or self-worth. Baxter's billions were used foremost to serve himself, despite what his philanthropic efforts might be.

Cal didn't feel anger for the man, just a raw sadness for the world that it should have to contend with men like Baxter.

"So, tell me, who am I dealing with, Mr. Baxter?" Cal asked.

He expected a torrent of lies to spew from the man's mouth, deluded thoughts brought on by a lifetime of percolating narcissism.

"I'm just like you, Mister —?"

"Stokes. Cal Stokes."

"I'm just like you, Mr. Stokes, a patriot and a warrior fighting for the betterment of my country."

"So, that's why you came up with this plan to wage war against the United States?"

Baxter's eyes twinkled with merriment.

"Oh. Oh, this is very good. You really don't know, do you?"

There was something in the man's tone that Cal didn't like. He saw Neil look up from where he was working on the computer they'd nabbed from Baxter's escape craft. Neil was confused too and Cal took a moment to try to read his friend's face.

Baxter clapped his hands together despite the cuffed wrists and pointed at Neil.

"See. Tell him, my friend. Tell Mr. Stokes my little secret."

Neil looked down at the computer screen and then back up to his friend in utter disbelief.

"What is it?" Cal asked. Neil's expression was more disconcerting than Baxter's glee.

Neil shook his head and then said, "He works for the CIA, Cal."

"Wait, what?" He must have misheard. Maybe the salt

water was clogging his ears or maybe the breach charge had dampened his hearing.

"It's all here. He's been working for the CIA for years. It was their idea to put this operation together."

As Cal's mind spun down the dark path of possibilities, Chance Baxter laughed at them. He roared as if it were the funniest thing he'd ever heard. When he finally settled down, he smiled at Cal and said, "Now that you know the truth, why don't you go along and inform the CIA that you have me in custody? I cannot wait to see what happens next."

Cal didn't move. Everything suddenly became clear. He remembered what the others had told him about Brandon's speech at the U.N. He remembered Travis going on endlessly about the broken political process. He remembered who he was.

"Well, I don't have all day," Baxter said, irritated now. Cal grinned. "Oh, I see, this is where you act tough and tell me what a shit I've been. Go ahead and get it out, Mr. Stokes. I am sure you have plenty to say about my carte blanche status, about how ironic it is that your government allows me to kill - so many I've killed. Yet all the while they keep you chained to a stake. It is fun, you know. I live the life of a socialite by day while playing 007 by night." He chuckled. And then he traced his bottom lip with his finger and mused, "What I wouldn't give to have seen the looks on your friends' faces as they plunged into the roiling sea."

Cal's smile disappeared.

Baxter cocked his head in amusement. "Ah, so you haven't found them – such a pity."

Cal brought up his weapon. It would never end. Baxter had learned to skirt the law and the law had given him every-thing he wanted. Some asshole in the CIA was going to get his due. However, the handler would probably just make excuses for the power they'd given Baxter. But Cal was no longer listening; it had to stop.

"I'm sorry, Mr. Baxter, you must have me mistaken for someone who actually gives a damn."

Baxter's mouth was just opening to respond when the burst from Cal's weapon tore into his face. Baxter fell back over the chair in which he previously been seated. There he remained lying motionless.

No one moved. Then there was commotion coming from the hallway. Top burst in, Maya's unconscious form cradled in his huge arms. He had cuts all over his face and along his arms. Daniel arrived virtually unscathed with Gaucho's arms draped over his shoulders. The Hispanic was grumbling something about water and how he would never go on a boat again.

"What happened?" Top asked, laying Maya gently on a couch.

Neil and the TJG operators who'd just witnessed the altercation remained speechless. Everyone was waiting for Cal to speak; finally, he did.

"I took out the trash."

Trent looked down at Baxter's body and then back at Cal. He put out his hand and Cal accepted it gratefully.

From behind them Daniel whispered, "Welcome back, Cal."

EPILOGUE

Wild Dunes

They gathered where Cal's rebirth began. After laying their fallen comrade to rest, they'd flown back as a family to the beach. Some were broken and bloodied, but they were all happy to be together again. Even Diane had flown in with Dr. Higgins.

Another memorial meant another opportunity to celebrate life. Finally, they had a few moments to relax after the potentially cataclysmic events of one week prior.

With the combined efforts of Neil's technical expertise and Chance Baxter's mighty ego, they'd unearthed the remaining pieces of the plot. Dr. Nahas filled in what details he knew, namely that his exploration vehicles had been retrofitted to carry different cargo. When Neil told him the cargo consisted of nuclear warheads, the doctor had withdrawn completely. His innovation, a tool intended to scour the depths of the oceans and unearth hidden treasures for his homeland, had been stolen and twisted to fulfill the evil desires of supposed patriots.

It hadn't taken much digging to find Baxter's CIA contact either. For someone with his intellect, Baxter truly believed that he was going to walk away a free man. Years of employ from a single handler at the CIA had given him that cocky assurance that he would remain untouchable.

When the director of the CIA found out that one of his top advisors, not only a good friend but also a fellow field agent with him during the eighties was the driving force behind the plot, he tendered his resignation on the spot.

When President Zimmer told the British and Israeli prime ministers of their countries' intelligence agencies' roles in the operation, they more forcefully demanded the resignations of the heads of MI6 and Shin Bet. The resignations were received; the world moved on.

Both prime ministers called to personally apologize. Zimmer's British counterpart had gone to the extent of offering Baxter's island to the Americans. The president said he would take it under advisement, informing The Jefferson Group that it might make a handy getaway for their covert team.

The plan had been quite simple. Barring interference, Baxter's yachts would launch Dr. Nahas's creations and the metal beasts would crawl to predesignated locations off the coast of every major power in the world. Then, with the weapons hidden, and the delivery vehicles only needing an occasional boost in power, subtle whispers would find their way to the ears of leaders worldwide. Who wouldn't listen to a rumor that nuclear missiles lay within easy shot of their nation's capitol? Thankfully, that didn't happen.

They got lucky with Baxter's yachts. It wasn't until Neil uncovered the chain of correspondence between the billionaire and the yacht captains that they found out, with much relief, the yachts weren't moving. They'd been ordered to sit tight and that's where they'd remained.

The yachts were taken down by American, British and Israeli special forces. Only one crew put up a fight. All the nuclear warheads were recovered.

Efraim Perlstein was in Israeli custody. The confessions flowed after being informed his side had lost. For all his bluster, Perlstein developed a humble streak in record time. His minions were being rounded up and the complete picture was coming together.

Hannah Krygier and Maya Eilenberg had been reunited. Maya, during her fall to the ocean, sustained a serious concussion. She was being monitored by President Zimmer's own physicians at Walter Reed until she could be released from the physician's care. Her Aunt Hannah hadn't left her side. From Maya's bedside, she had briefed her brother, the contrite Israeli Prime Minister. Krygier hadn't known much of what Perlstein's plan involved. However, the information she did know was willingly shared. This assisted the Israelis in asking Perlstein the correct questions.

So, as they soaked in the late summer rays under the blazing hot sun, the men of The Jefferson Group had much to be thankful for. Most importantly, they had their leader back. Cal had returned from his sojourn with a worldly gaze. To his men, and especially to Daniel, Cal seemed calmer now. The sniper smiled at that as he watched Cal and Diane chase Liberty down the beach, the puppy running away with a dead fish that had washed ashore. Daniel laughed and sipped from the plastic water bottle. Such days were few and far between. Luckily, Daniel knew how to enjoy them and he had a pretty good feeling that now Cal did, too.

THE WHITE HOUSE: 3:35PM

The cameras were rolling and Ken Wick flashed his rehearsed smile at the camera. He was still in command of *The Ludlow*

Report, courtesy of the fact its host had contracted a stomach bug during his Caribbean cruise. It was all gravy for Wick, whose star had continued to rise and now seemed to be reaching a new pinnacle, as he sat across from President Brandon Zimmer.

"Welcome back. Before our break, President Zimmer and I were discussing the challenges he's faced in his first term in the Oval Office. Now if it's okay with you, Mr. President, I'd like to delve into something everyone's talking about. Might you guess what I'm alluding to?"

Zimmer smiled warmly at his interviewer.

"Let me guess, you want to talk about The Zimmer Doctrine." It was said, almost in jest. Wick knew the president didn't like to talk about it. His sources said Zimmer disliked the use of his name in conjunction with the doctrine. In a cynical town like Washington, Wick didn't believe a word of it.

"Yes, Mr. President. *The Zimmer Doctrine*. There's been a lot of speculation about exactly what it is and how you plan to implement it. I'd like to ask you to describe The Zimmer Doctrine in a single word."

Wick expected the president to play word games and dodge his question. It's what so many politicians did and they were good at it.

But, much to Wick's surprise, the president did not hesitate.

"Ownership," Zimmer said.

Wick couldn't find the words to respond for a long moment. He'd been ready to pounce. Now his ploy had backfired.

"Ownership?" Wick asked. "Could you elaborate?"

Wick saw his producer behind the cameraman. He was grinning at Wick's gaffe which he tried to ignore.

"Of course," Zimmer said. "I've learned a lot about taking

ownership of my actions. I am fortunate to have surrounded myself with friends and advisors who are never afraid to call me out when I am wrong or make bad decisions. It can be very humbling and frustrating, but I believe it has made me a better and more effective leader. What I've come to realize is that my legacy will be based on one thing and it isn't how many Twitter followers I have. My legacy will be built on my reputation, as both a man and as a leader. It is my sincere hope that history judges me not only by the things I've done right, but also by the fact that I have owned up to my mistakes, America's mistakes, and my attempts to fix them."

"Is this what led you to give your speech at the United Nations where you basically accused the world of taking advantage of America's goodwill?"

Zimmer smiled patiently. "I believe if you go back and listen to what I said, you'll find that I pointed a finger at the world, but I also told the world that America would have to take a long look at itself in the mirror. You see, Ken, we've done a lot of good things around the world. We've helped countries that wanted and needed our help. But we've also made some big mistakes. One of the most egregious is that we've tried to implement our own ideology in cultures and settings that would probably be better served in a different way."

"Could you give us an example, Mr. President?" Wick felt the reins slipping out of his hands. Zimmer was good. More than that, Wick saw that it wasn't bullshit. The president really believed his convictions.

"The best example is one we've given serious thought to. For a long time, we've tried to bring democracy to the world. We have waved the flag of freedom and promised a new life if only countries would embrace the American political model. But, here's the problem. We're all different. What works here may not work in a developing country. They may not be ready or they may not have the capability to run things the way we do. Their leadership may say they're ready because we've promised all this aid, but maybe, just maybe, we should look deeper and spend more time listening to their needs. Perhaps they have the answer and we need to stop placing our beliefs on them. You can't make a centuries-old system change, but you can plant the seeds of freedom and tolerance and then work with that country's people to see what grows. I'm here to say that we've been wrong in the past, and we'll undoubtedly be wrong in the future. However, as long as I am president, I will seek to do what is right, rather than what is popular."

"I think we've heard that line countless times before, Mr. President. Don't you think it's a little naive to imagine a world where everyone lives by the Golden Rule?"

The president stared at him for a long moment and smiled again.

"It might make me appear naive, Ken, but I'd rather be naive and hopeful than bitter and vengeful. Imagine what would happen if politicians truly took their constituents' best interests at heart and stopped using scare tactics to sway votes."

"That's a bold thing to say considering you have a re-election coming up."

Zimmer shrugged like he didn't care.

"Believe what you want, Ken, but I'm taking my administration to task and I'm requesting that Congress work with me on this. It won't be easy but I think it's the right thing to do."

Wick thought he saw an in, but the clock in the corner informed him he had time to address only one more subject.

"One last question, Mr. President. How do you think this new approach bodes for your chances of re-election?"

President Zimmer's smile was even wider this time.

"I guess we'll just have to see."

* * *

I hope you enjoyed this story.
If you did, please take a moment to write a review <u>ON AMAZON</u>. Even the short ones help!

GET A FREE COPY OF THE CORPS JUSTICE PREQUEL SHORT STORY, *GOD-SPEED*, JUST FOR SUBSCRIBING AT <u>CG-COOPER.COM</u>

MORE THANKS TO MY BETA READERS:

Sue, Cheryl, Susan, Wanda, Glenda, Don, Pat, Terry, David, Andrea, Mary, CaryLory, Robert, Nancy, Bob, Julie, Richard, Marsha, Kathryn, Michael, Chip and John. You all keep this ship from sinking.

ALSO BY C. G. COOPER

Broken

Tested

The Tom Greer Novels

A Life Worth Taking

The Spy In Residence Novels

What Lies Hidden

The Alex Knight Novels:

Breakout

The Stars & Spies Series:

Backdrop

The Patriot Protocol Series:

The Patriot Protocol

The Chronicles of Benjamin Dragon:

Benjamin Dragon – Awakening

Benjamin Dragon – Legacy

Benjamin Dragon - Genesis

ABOUT THE AUTHOR

C. G. Cooper is the USA TODAY and AMAZON
BESTSELLING author of the CORPS JUSTICE novels
(including spinoffs), The Chronicles of Benjamin Dragon and
the Patriot Protocol series.

Cooper grew up in a Navy family and traveled from one
Naval base to another as he fed his love of books and a
fledgling desire to write.

Upon graduating from the University of Virginia with a
degree in Foreign Affairs, Cooper was commissioned in the

United States Marine Corps and went on to serve six years as an infantry officer. C. G. Cooper's final Marine duty station was in Nashville, Tennessee, where he fell in love with the laid-back lifestyle of Music City.

His first published novel, BACK TO WAR, came out of a need to link back to his time in the Marine Corps. That novel, written as a side project, spawned many follow-on novels, several exciting spinoffs, and catapulted Cooper's career.

Cooper lives just south of Nashville with his wife, three children, and their German shorthaired pointer, Liberty, who's become a popular character in the Corps Justice novels.

When he's not writing or hosting his podcast, Books In 30, Cooper spends time with his family, does his best to improve his golf handicap, and loves to shed light on the ongoing fight of everyday heroes.

Cooper loves hearing from readers and responds to every email personally.

To connect with C. G. Cooper visit
www.cg-cooper.com

MEDIAPOLIS PUBLIC LIBRARY
128 N. ORCHARD ST.
MEDIAPOLIS, IA 52637

64861719R00140

Made in the USA
Columbia, SC
12 July 2019